Conversational English Alive

情境英语
速成会话

萧 珮 编著

含MP3
光盘

华东理工大学出版社

用图画带入英语情境，用故事串联生活英语

轻松用英语和外国人聊天

　　学英语的目的不在考试拿高分，而是要有能力和外国人沟通。如果英语能力只停留在纸上谈兵，实际面对外国人时，却一句话也说不出来，那不是白学了吗？

　　还有许多人由于学校的应试教育，背了一大堆平常用不到的单词和不符合口语的句子，就算在考试中拿了高分，实际和外国人聊天时，只能说出How are you? Fine, Thank you, and you? 之类的对话。如果不能聊出点"东西"来，只知道该怎么打招呼，这样怎么能够沟通呢？

　　本书特别针对和外国人聊天社交时一定会用到的30个情境会话，不但囊括衣、食、住、行等生活基本情境，更有传达情绪、警告、借钱等实用情境，学会了这些情境会话，就能轻松和外国人谈天说笑，介绍中国文化，甚至让老板对你的英语能力刮目相看！

　　除了完整的内容外，本书还有五大法宝，让您轻松成为英语社交达人：

1. 图像式学习，融入英语情境

运用图像联系情境，学英文不再枯燥，让您在各种场合都能展开联想，在潜意识中加强学习效果。

2. 拟真情境，绝对实用

30个一定会用到的社交情境，模拟真实情况，配合拟真录音，说出最恰当的英语社交辞令。

3. 最地道的用法

介绍在学校学不到的实用英语，翻遍课本也找不到的地道用法，说一口漂亮精准的英语。

4. 关键单词，灵活运用

一网打尽社交时会用到的关键单词，只要熟记这些单词，遇到什么情况都能应付自如。

5. 重点句型，说出最流利的社交英语

要说出流利的英语，就要学好句型，把句型内化成语感，面对外国人也能侃侃而谈。

只要跟着本书的步骤，结合图像、文字和语音教学，必定能够说一口有内容的好英语，轻松和外国人聊天！

男主角: Luke, 24岁

女主角: Rose, 22岁

您好，我是Luke，从小到大都没出过国，去过最远的地方是绿岛，这回居然跟个外国人当室友，真是让我超级紧张，希望我们不会沟通不良。我之前任职于某家电脑公司，人称"网络工程师"，现在我决定自己当老板，至于为什么，嘿嘿，看下去就知道了。对了，我还有个漂亮的女朋友Rose，可别太羡慕我啰！

嗨，我是Rose，今年22岁。我是某大学的大四学生，专修服装设计。课余闲暇，我也接兼职的模特儿工作，充实荷包。等大学毕业后，我准备到纽约学服装设计。最近我男朋友有了一个外国室友Robert，常常有一些搞笑的事情，让我的日子增添不少趣味。

男主角: Robert, 25岁

女主角: Jessica, 23岁

Hello, my name is Robert. In the book, it seems that I make a lot of troubles, and sometimes make scenes in public. Well, it is not the way I usually do, you know. If you know me better, you'll find that I am a very serious guy. Anyway, thanks for buying this book.

呼！单身了好几年，人称 Miss Particular的我，终于在今年……，先卖个关子，等各位看完这本书就了解啰！

同学甲: Simon, 24岁　　**同学乙: Linda, 30岁**

大家好，我是Simon，Robert的同学。我们一起在师大语文中心学中文，我来台湾已经两年了，等大学毕业后，即将前往大陆经营精油的生意。

Hello，我是西班牙人Linda。我跟Simon他们一样，也是来台湾学习中文的，大学英文系毕业后，我就选择来台湾教英文。我发现台湾是个有趣的地方。现在，我有个台湾男友，交往还算顺利。

同事甲: Peter, 25岁

同事乙: Chen, 36岁

大家好，我是Peter，也是Luke的同事。

哈啰，我是Miss Chen。我是Robert的女上司，也是所属公司的首席设计师，为人面冷心善。你们看了我工作时果决的表现，可不要偷偷喜欢上我喔！

同事丙: Tiffany, 22岁

同学丙: Lily, 24岁

我是和Robert同公司的电脑程序设计师，我人生最大的目的就是工作，他们都说我是个工作狂。什么？你问我这种生活会不会很无趣，其实还好啦！至少现在有了这位有时少根筋的Robert，让我工作时的紧张情绪放松了不少。

别搞错了，我是Luke的高中同学。很不幸，我的镜头很少，只出现一次，希望大家不要太快把我忘记了。

Content

情境英语速成会话

目录

情境英语速成会话　Content

Unit 1
Are you looking for a roommate?
询问房租&看房子

Luke's roommate moves out, so he has to look for a new roommate. He posts the information on the Internet, and many people replied to it. To his surprise, a foreigner comes to knock at his door. Oh, my! Luke never has gotten good grades on his English tests. How does he talk and have an interview with the foreigner? Do you think they will become roommates?

Luke的室友搬走了，所以他得找一个新室友。他将信息张贴在网络上，不少人登门面试。没想到，还有金发碧眼的外国人呢！天啊，以前Luke英文考试都是低分飞过。你想，他要怎么跟"阿逗啊"面试？他们两人会不会成为室友呢？

现在是什么情况?

(The doorbell is ringing. Luke goes to answer the door. To his surprise, outside stands a foreigner.)

Robert: Hi, I'm Robert Golden. You must be Luke Chen.

Luke: How do you do?

Robert: How do you do?

Luke: Nice to meet you.

Robert: Nice to meet you, too. I heard that you have your house for rent, don't you?

（门铃响了，卢克去开门。没想到，门外竟然站着一个外国人。）

罗伯特：嗨，我是罗伯特·戈尔登。你一定是陈卢克了。

卢　克：初次见面，你好。

罗伯特：初次见面，你好。

卢　克：很高兴见到你。

罗伯特：我也很高兴见到你。听说你有房子要出租，有这回事吗？

Luke: In fact, it isn't my own house. I'm just looking for a roommate. How did you know about it?

Robert: I'm very interested in the ad you posted on the Internet, so I came here to see and talk to you. Can you show me around the house?

Luke: Sure, come on in. This is a two-bedroom apartment, and it is well-furnished. All are modern conveniences. Above all, it's not too expensive for rent.

Robert: How much is the rent?

Luke: NT$6,000 per month, including electricity. Only one month rent for deposit. If you want to move out, just give me a thirty-day notice, and I'll return the deposit.

Robert: Not bad.

卢　克：事实上，那不是我自己的房子。我只是在找室友。你怎么知道的？

罗伯特：我对你登在网络上的广告很感兴趣，所以就来看看，顺便跟你聊聊。可以带我看看房子吗？

卢　克：当然，快进来。这是一间两房的公寓，设备齐全。都是现代化设备。最重要的是，房租不贵。

罗伯特：房租多少？

卢　克：每月新台币六千块，含电费。押金只要一个月的租金。若要搬出去，三十天前通知我，我便会退还押金。

罗伯特：还不赖嘛！

Unit 1 询问房租 & 看房子
情境英语速成会话

必备活用单词

❶ rent：当名词，可解释为"租金、出租的财产"。

◀ ... for rent 表示"某物要出租"，在英国，我们在广告上会看见英国人将 House For Rent 写成 House To Let，跟美国人不一样喔！

❷ ad：就是advertisement"广告"的缩写。

❸ post：这是最近很流行的网络术语，意思是"张贴、发表"。

◀ 此外，它还有"标竿、电线杆、足球的门柱"之意。翻开词典，其实你会发现post这个单词很有趣，例如post office是"邮局"；在post后多加了er，就成了poster"海报"。

❹ show ... around ...："带某人逛某地方"。

◀ 其他常用的词组有show up和show off；前者是"出现"，后者是"故意炫耀"之意，请不要搞错了。

❺ two-bedroom apartment："两房公寓"。

◀ 若我们想说"三房一厅"，可说成three-bedroom and one living room即可。至于"单人房"，就是single-room了。

❻ well-furnished："装潢好的，附家具的"，形容词。furnish是动词，本身有"给房间配置家具或装潢"之意。

❼ modern conveniences：modern是"现代的、摩登的"；convenience有"便利的设施、方便的用具"之意。

◀ 在英国convenience也有"公厕"之意。

❽ above all：“最重要的”、“首先”的意思。

❾ electricity：“电力”，此处指“电费”。

◀ utility在美国常指“公共事业”，如电、煤气、自来水等。而 utilities则是我们所謂的“水电费”之意。

❿ deposit：“押金”的意思。

◀ 若用在银行，则指“存款、存钱”。

⑪ 30-day notice：“三十天前告知”。

◀ 在租房契约上常有这一条，房客必须在搬家前三十天通知房东，才能退还押金。这三十天前的通知，英文就是thirty-day notice。

What's next? 结果如何呢?

(After looking around, Robert sits on the sofa in the living room. Luke is making coffee for his guest.)

Robert: I've been looking for an apartment of this kind for a long time. To tell you the truth, I really love this kitchen and beautiful views here.

Luke: That's why I moved in when I found it. It's quite nice, isn't it?

Robert: That's a bargain!

Luke: When will you move in? Have it your own way.

Robert: I'll move in next Monday.

Luke: If you need any help, just give me a call.

Robert: Thanks.

Unit 1 询问房租&看房子
情境英语速成会话

（看完房子后，罗伯特坐在客厅的沙发上。卢克正在泡咖啡招待客人。）

罗伯特：我找像这样的房子已经好久了。说实话，我真的很喜欢这里的厨房和漂亮的景色。

卢　克：这就是为什么我找到这房子就搬进来的原因。这里很不错，不是吗？

罗伯特：就这么说定了！

卢　克：你什么时候搬进来？一切随你方便。

罗伯特：我想下星期一搬进来好了。

卢　克：若你需要帮忙，打个电话给我。

罗伯特：谢了。

 句型

1. How do you do?	幸会

对于初次见面的人，我们不用"How are you?"，而是用"How do you do?"。这句话，中文翻译成"初次见面，幸会"，或简洁一点，直接翻译成"幸会"就可以了。听到这句话的人，肯定也是初次碰到对方，自然也得讲"How do you do?"。

2. If + 从句，从句   如果／要是……，就……

表示某种条件，我们常使用带if的条件从句。例如：If it rains, I won't go to school.（要是下雨了，我就不去学校）。所以，不去学校的条件是"下雨"。这样，清楚条件从句的用法了吗？

这样说最地道！

影片中，我们看到英美人士的小屋子（house）前都有个小庭院（garden），外头是修剪整齐的篱笆（fence）或树篱（hedge），让人非常羡慕。其实，大部分住在都市的人可没这么好运，他们大多住在公寓。英国的公寓叫flat，美国的叫apartment；分户出租的小公寓房子叫condo。另外，在巨星云集的好莱坞，常可在报上见某某人又买了大豪宅（villa）或到某小岛的度假小屋（cottage）度假，令人大叹上帝不公平。

 这个单元的内容都记熟了吗？继续加油，准备前往下一个单元啰！

Unit 1 询问房租＆看房子
情境英语速成会话

Unit 2
You're a good bargain-hunter.

如何请求帮忙 & 如何杀价

At last, Luke finds a new roommate. You're right—
his roommate is that foreigner, Robert. Robert's
TV set is out of order, and he asks Luke to buy
a cheap one with him in the flea market in the
night market. To buy a cheap but wonderful TV,
do you know how Luke uses his poor English
to help Robert to bargain?

Luke终于找到新室友了。没错，就是那个"阿逗啊"——Robert。Robert的电视机坏掉了，他请Luke带他到夜市的跳蚤市场买便宜货。你想知道英文很蹩脚的Luke，怎么和他的室友联合杀价，买了一台物美价廉的电视机吗？

现在是什么情况?

(There is a very loud noise from Robert's room. Luke is going to see what happens.)

Luke: What's wrong with your TV? It makes a lot of noise.

Robert: I think it's out of order.

Luke: How come? It looks quite new.

Robert: Who knows? I'm repairing it, but it's getting worse and worse. Oh, what should I do? I really need a TV to learn Chinese.

（罗伯特的房间传来非常嘈杂的噪音。卢克去看看到底发生什么事情了。）

卢　克：你的电视机怎么了？它很吵耶！

罗伯特：我想电视机可能坏掉了。

卢　克：怎么会呢？它看起来挺新的。

罗伯特：谁知道？我正在修理它，可是情况越来越糟糕。喔，我该怎么办呢？我可非常需要一台电视来学中文。

22

Luke: Why don't you buy a new one? A brand-new TV is no more than NT$15,000.

Robert: Well, I want to, but I have a tight budget.

Luke: Don't worry. I know some night markets selling cheap stuff. Although they're second-hand, and they don't have gorgeous appearances, they're worth buying.

Robert: Could you tell me where the night markets are? I'll head for them after class.

Luke: Take it easy. I'll go with you and have dinner there.

Robert: Maybe you can teach me how to bargain with those traders.

Luke: It's a piece of cake. Here is a tip. Repeat after me: "The price is too high, and I need to think". It works every time.

Robert: You must be kidding.

卢　克：怎么不买台新的？一台全新的电视机不超过一万五千块新台币。

罗伯特：嗯，我是想要买，可是我的手头有点紧。

卢　克：别担心。我知道有些夜市卖便宜货。它们虽然是二手的，看起来也不怎么样，可是物超所值。

罗伯特：可以告诉我夜市在哪里吗？我下课后就直接到那里去。

卢　克：放轻松点。我会跟你一块去，顺便在那儿吃晚餐。

罗伯特：或许你可以教我怎么跟那些摊贩杀价。

Unit 2 如何请求帮忙＆如何杀价
情境英语速成会话

卢　克：小意思。秘诀在此——跟我重复这些话："价格太贵了，我考虑一下。"这一招每次都奏效。

罗伯特：你一定是在开玩笑。

 ## 必备活用单词

❶ noise：名词，解释为"噪音"，所有不悦耳的声音都叫 noise。

◀ make a noise 表示"制造噪音"。

❷ order：名词，表示"次序、状况"。

◀ out of order 表示"状况不好"，也就是"坏掉了"之意。

❸ worse and worse：形容词，可表示任何情况"越来越糟"。

❹ brand-new：形容词，表示"全新的、崭新的"。

❺ budget：名词，表示"预算"。

◀ have a tight budget 表示"手头很紧、预算不充裕"。

❻ gorgeous：形容词，用于口语表示"极好的"。

❼ appearance：名词，表示"外表"。

❽ head for：动词词组，表示"前往"。

❾ bargain：动词，表示"讨价还价、杀价"。

◀ bargain with + 人，表示"和（某人）讨价还价"。

 ## What's next? 结果如何呢？

(Robert picks out the TV he likes and is bargaining with a trader.)

Robert: How much is this one?

Trader: NT$3,500.

Robert: Too much, lou-bian. I don't have so much money with me. Can you give me a discount?

Trader: Sorry, it is quite cheap.

Robert: Come on, this is all the money I have, NT$3,170.

Trader: Well, you're a good bargain hunter.

 中文翻译

（**罗伯特选了自己喜欢的电视机，现在正在跟摊贩杀价。**）

罗伯特：这台多少钱？

小　贩：新台币3 500元。

罗伯特：太贵了，老板。我身上没带那么多钱。可以算我便宜一点吗？

小　贩：对不起，这真的很便宜了。

Unit 2 如何请求帮忙＆如何杀价

情境英语速成会话

罗伯特：别这样，这是我所有的钱，才新台币3 170元而已。

小　贩：嗯，你可真会买便宜货。

必备活用单词

❶ discount：名词，"折扣"。

　◀ give ... a discount表示"给某人优惠"，也就是算某人便宜一
　　点的意思。

❷ bargain hunter：四处找便宜货买的人。

句型

worse and worse	越来越糟

关于比较级的用法，通常我们会在形容词的后面加上-er或在形容
词前加上more。可是，碰到bad的比较级就行不通了，它的比较级
和最高级分别是worse和worst。若要表示某情况每况愈下，可用
"It is getting worse and worse."。

这样说最地道！

说到杀价（bargain），除了艺高胆大之外，就是不能心软。也就是说，碰到该杀价的时候，一定得把"算我便宜一点"（give me a discount）、"有点太贵喔"（a little bit expensive），或"让我想想看"（let me think about it）这类的话挂在嘴上，让老板担心一下，才能把价格压下来。

这个单元的内容都记熟了吗？继续加油，准备前往下一个单元啰！

Unit 3
Don't make a mess, please.

如何传达警告之意&
如何下达命令

Luke and Robert stay together for a while, and they get along well with each other. However, Luke always messes up the kitchen. One day Robert finds a cockroach in the kitchen, and he is scared to death. Then, he asks Luke to clean it. Do you know how a Virgo like Robert asks Luke to sleeve up and clean the house?

相处一阵子，Luke和他的"阿逗啊"室友越来越默契了。不过，Luke总是把厨房弄得乱七八糟。有一天，Robert在厨房发现一只蟑螂，他吓得半死。之后，他便要求Luke展开大扫除。你知道处女座的Robert，如何让Luke和他一起卷起袖子打扫房子吗？

现在是什么情况?

(Robert stays up late for tomorrow's exam. After studying, he is looking for something to eat in the kitchen. Then, he can't help screaming out.)

Luke: Are you all right, Robert?

Robert: I was almost scared to death in the kitchen.

Luke: Did you see a burglar breaking into our house?

Robert: No, there're cockroaches drowning in my bowl.

Luke: How disgusting! That sight made my flesh creep.

Robert: Luke, I think I need to discuss something with you.

（罗伯特为了明天的考试而熬夜。苦读之后，他到厨房找吃的东西。接着，他就忍不住放声大叫。）

卢　克：你还好吧，罗伯特？

罗伯特：我在厨房快被吓死了。

卢　克：看见小偷了？

罗伯特：不是，是我碗里有蟑螂在爬。

卢　克：太恶心了。那情景让我起鸡皮疙瘩。

罗伯特：卢克，我觉得必须跟你好好谈一谈。

Luke: How come?

Robert: Our kitchen is filthy. It looks like it's been hit by a tornado. It's you who messes up the kitchen.

Luke: It's a very serious accusation. Are you sure about that, Robert?

Robert: A few days ago you forgot doing dishes after eating, and the next morning, there were ants and cockroaches everywhere.

The day before yesterday…

Luke: Oops, my mistake.

卢　克：为什么？

罗伯特：我们的厨房够脏的。看起来就像给龙卷风扫过一样。是你把厨房搞得乱七八糟。

卢　克：这可是非常严重的指控。罗伯特，你确定吗？

罗伯特：前几天吃完饭你忘了洗碗，隔天，到处是蚂蚁和蟑螂。

前天……

卢　克：哦，都是我的错。

必备活用单词

❶ stay up：动词词组，"熬夜"。

　◀ stay up late for ... 表示"为……熬夜"。

❷ scream out：动词词组，"大声尖叫"。

❸ scare：动词，"惊吓"。

　◀ be scared to death 表示"吓得半死"。

❹ burglar：名词，"窃贼"。

❺ break into：动词词组，"破门而入"。

❻ cockroach：名词，"蟑螂"。

❼ drown：动词，"溺水"。

❽ disgusting：形容词，"恶心的"。

❾ sight：名词，"景象"。

　◀ 此外，sight 还有"视力、风景、观光地"之意。

❿ flesh：名词，"肉体"。

　◀ 此处flesh指的是"全身"之意。

⑪ creep：动词，"起鸡皮疙瘩"。

◀ That sight makes my flesh creep. 表示"那景象让我全身起鸡皮疙瘩"。

⑫ discuss：动词，"讨论"。

◀ discuss... with + 人，表示"和某人讨论某事"。

⑬ filthy：形容词，"肮脏的，不洁的"。

⑭ tornado：名词，"龙卷风"。

◀ it's been hit by a tornado. 是"被龙卷风扫过"，用来形容房子非常凌乱。

⑮ mess up：动词，"弄乱"。

⑯ accusation：名词，"指控"。

What's next? 结果如何呢?

Luke: Is there anything I can do to make up for my carelessness?

Robert: Of course. How about cleaning up the kitchen tomorrow?

Luke: By my own? No way!

Robert: Don't panic. Cleaning up is very easy. For example, we can use potpourri packets to hide kitchen odors. In short, all you need to do is roll up your sleeves.

Luke: I haven't rolled up my sleeves in my whole life.

Robert: Then, tomorrow is a good chance, isn't it?

卢　克：我可以做什么来弥补我的粗心大意呢？

罗伯特：当然。明天把厨房好好打扫一下，如何？

卢　克：我自己一个人？不要！

罗伯特：别慌张。打扫非常容易。例如，我们可以用干燥花香包来
　　　　消除厨房臭味。总之一句话，你要做的就是卷起袖子。

卢　克：我这一生可还没卷起袖子过。

罗伯特：那明天可是大好机会，不是吗？

 必备活用单词

❶ make up：动词词组，"补偿、弥补"。

　◀ 此外，make up 还有"和某人破镜重圆、合好"之意。

❷ clean up：动词词组，"打扫干净"。

❸ by one's own：词组，"独自"。

❹ no way：词组，"绝不"。

❺ panic：动词，"惊慌失措"。

◀ Don't panic. 用来劝告某人不要惊慌失措，把心情镇定下来。

❻ potpourri：名词，"干燥花"。

◀ 此外，此单词还有"杂烩、杂文集"之意。

❼ packet：名词，"包"。

❽ roll up：动词词组，"卷起"。

◀ roll 通常用来表示"卷状物"，例如：一卷面包、一卷羊皮纸等等。

❾ sleeve：名词，"袖子"。

 句型

1. can't help + V-ing	忍不住……

日常生活中，许多人的口头禅可能是"我忍不住要……"。这"忍不住"不是想上厕所的忍不住，而是克制不住某种欲望的意思，请不要搞错啰！而英文的"忍不住"必须用"can't help + V-ing"和"can't help but + V"来表示。两者最大的差异在于help后得用名词或动名词；而but之后是用动词原形。例如："I did it because I couldn't help it."（无可奈何，我只好做了。）、"She couldn't help but laugh."（她忍不住大笑起来。）

2. (It's) a good chance to ... （去做某事的）大好机会

"大好机会"是我们常听见的一句话。机会（chance）我们是知道的，那表示做某事情的大好机会呢？这时，我们就得用句型"it is + a good chance + to + V"，如："It's a good chance to win her back."（那是再度获得她芳心的大好机会。）。若要加上对某人是大好机会呢？只要在句子中加入for + someone即可。如上面的例子："It's a good chance for John to win her back."。

这样说最地道！

说到打扫，真的不像Robert所言如此简单，只要一个干花包（potpourri packet）便可解决。如此看来，Robert一定是故意骗Luke上贼船。想想看，打扫的行头（cleaning supplies）那么多，例如：鸡毛掸子（feather duster）、吸尘器（vacuum cleaner）、水桶（bucket）、拖把（wet mop）、抹布（rag）、清洁剂（detergent），光是准备这些工具就够累人的，不是吗？

Unit 4
Here's the electricity bill.
如何和对方讨论金钱&
如何描述节约

It is so hot that Robert, from North America, can't stand the heat in the summer. So, he stays in his air-conditioned home all day long. Today the mailman takes the electricity bill to him, and tells him: "The sum of the electricity fee is so high that you can buy two more air conditioners with it." Oh, my God. What's going on? Robert is very nervous and he will discuss how to save money with Luke after he comes home. Do you know what their ideas are?

夏天到了，来自美国北方的Robert热得晕头转向，
只好整天躲在自家的空调房不出门。没想到今天邮
差先生送来了电费账单，还好心地告诉他——他们
家的电费可以买两台空调了。老天啊，怎么会这
样？紧张的Robert一等Luke下班，便和他商量抢救
账单大作战。你知道他们会想出什么好点子吗？

现在是什么情况?

Robert: Here is our bill for utilities. Do you want to have a look?

Luke: I smell a rat. Tell me, what do you have in mind?

Robert: We need to pay over NT$10,000 for the bill.

Luke: You don't say. Why is it like that?

Robert: I have no idea myself, either. Maybe I let the air conditioner run too long.

Luke: What do you mean?

罗伯特：这是我们的水电费账单。你想看看吗?

卢　克：有点可疑喔！告诉我，你在想什么?

罗伯特：我们的账单是新台币一万多块。

卢　克：不会吧！怎么会这样?

罗伯特：我自己也不知道。可能是我让空调开太久了。

卢　克：什么意思?

Robert: Well, I stay home for at least eight hours a day during the summer vacation. In such hot weather, you know, I can't live without an air conditioner. It's like fish out of water.

Luke: I see your point, but it's a lot of money. Let me think.

Robert: I have some solutions: During the daytime, I'll stay in the library, or other places that have air conditioning. When I sleep, I will open the door instead.

Luke: That's a good idea.

Robert: Then, I'll call a plumber to see if our air conditioner is too old. Maybe it's a leak problem.

Luke: You're right.

罗伯特：嗯，这暑假我每天待在家超过八小时以上。这样热的天气，没有空调我受不了，就像鱼离开了水一样。

卢　克：我了解，但是那可是不便宜啊。让我想想。

罗伯特：我有解决的方法了：白天的时候我会待在图书馆，或任何有空调的地方。睡觉的时候，我就开窗户好了。

卢　克：好主意！

罗伯特：然后，我会打电话给水电工，看看我们的空调是否太旧了。也有可能是漏电。

卢　克：没错。

必备活用单词

❶ bill：名词，"账单"。

　　◀ 除了当账单外，此单词还有"目录、节目清单、法案、钞票"之意。

❷ utilities：名词，"公共事业"，如水电、煤气、电话等。

　　◀ utility 比较常用在"效用、实用之物"等意义上。

❸ I smell a rat：我觉得可疑。

　　◀ 别怀疑，"闻到老鼠的味道"就是"可疑"之意。

❹ air conditioner：名词，"空调"。

　　◀ 由此单词所延伸的单词尚有：air-conditioned（形容词，装有空调的）、air-condition（动词，用空调调节）。

❺ live without：动词词组，"要活下去不能没有⋯⋯"。

❻ it's like fish out of water："格格不入"。

❼ figure out：动词词组，"想出、理解"。

❽ solution：名词，"解决方法"。

❾ plumber：名词，"水电工人"。

⑩ leak：名词，"漏（水、电、煤气等）"。

◀ it's a leak problem 表示"那是漏电的问题"。

What's next? 结果如何呢?

Luke: It's hot in your room, Robert. How can you stand it?

Robert: I want to save money, so I turn off the air conditioner to make a difference.

Luke: Don't be so harsh. It's just a matter of money. Nobody expects you to live in hell. Turn on the air conditioner.

Robert: Thanks. You're really a good buddy.

中文翻译

卢　克：罗伯特，你的房间热死了。你怎么受得了？

罗伯特：我想要省钱啊，所以我把空调关了。

卢　克：别这么苛刻。只不过是钱的问题。没人希望你住在地狱受苦受难。把空调打开啦！

罗伯特：谢啦。你真是个好人。

句型

1. instead　　作为代替

instead 这个单词有"选择某物作为替代、取而代之"的意思，因为这个单词不是动词，只是副词，所以大多放在句尾。例如："When I sleep, I will open the window instead."。而instead of 则有"而非……"，用法跟上面不同，例如："I gave my brother a book instead of a computer." (我给我弟弟一本书，而非一台电脑。)，也可等于"I gave my brother a book instead."。

2. It's jus a mater of ...　　只不过是……的问题

matter 本身有"事件、问题"之意，所以"it is a matter of..."代表"是……的问题"，在句子中多放了just就有"只不过是……的问题"，此可解释为"大不了是……"。例如："It's a matter of money." (是钱的问题。)、"a matter of life and death" (攸关生死的问题)。

这样说最地道！

古人说："长安居，大不易"。其实，一个地方的生活水准（living standard）会影响我们养家糊口的能力。住在乡下地方，那些日常开销费用（living expense），如房租（rent）、电话费（telephone bill）、水电费（electricity bill）、娱乐费（amusement expense）会比较省喔！

Unit 4 如何和对方讨论金钱 & 如何描述节约
情境英语速成会话

Unit 5
How do you want your hair done?
如何询问发型

Robert's hair is too long and it makes him look
like a gang member. Luke suggests that he have
a hair cut. Robert's classmates, Simon and
Linda, introduce him to a good barber. With
their help, he has a gorgeous new look.

Robert的头发太长了，看起来真像混帮派的，Luke建议他赶紧把头发剪了。Robert的同班同学，Simon和Linda介绍他一个优秀的理发师。有了Simon和Linda的帮忙，他和理发师沟通良好，剪了一个超酷的发型，真是帅呆了！

现在是什么情况?

(They enter the barber's. Linda is discussing with the barber in Chinese about Robert's hair.)

Linda: Mr. Yang asked how you want your hair done?

Robert: Can he give it a good trimming?

Simon: You mean cut it short all around? Or, just take a little bit off the sides and at the back?

Robert: Well, good question. I'd like a crew cut.

（他们进入理发店。琳达用中文跟理发师讨论罗伯特的头发。）

琳　达：杨先生问你，你想要怎么处理你的头发呢？

罗伯特：可以请他好好修剪一下吗？

西　蒙：你是指全部剪短？还是，只在两侧和后面稍微修一下？

罗伯特：嗯，问得好。我想要理平头。

Linda:	Are you sure? It might make you look like a prisoner.
Robert:	I don't mind. It's burning outsides during the summertime here.
Linda:	Would you like some hair conditioner? It's good for the scalp, and it prevents dandruff.
Robert:	No, thanks. It's not my style, and it sounds a little sissy.
Linda:	How about a shave or a shampoo?
Robert:	How much does a shave or a shampoo cost?
Simon:	Free.
Robert:	Why not?

· ·

中文翻译

琳　达：	不会吧？那会使你看起来像囚犯。
罗伯特：	我才不介意。这里夏天外头简直热得像火烤一样。
琳　达：	想要护发素吗？那对头皮不错，还可预防头皮屑。
罗伯特：	不，谢了。那不是我的行事风格，听起来有点娘娘腔。
琳　达：	那刮个胡子或洗个头呢？
罗伯特：	刮胡子或洗头要多少钱？
西　蒙：	免费。
罗伯特：	那为何不要呢？

Unit 5 如何询问发型
情境英语速成会话

必备活用单词

❶ barber：名词，"理发师"。

　◀ 美发师是 "hairdresser"。

❷ trimming：名词，"修剪"。

　◀ trim 本身是动词，表示"修剪、整理"之意。

❸ crew cut：名词，"平头"。

❹ hair conditioner：名词，"护发素"、"润发乳"。

　◀ 洗发水为 "shampoo"。

❺ scalp：名词，"头皮"。

❻ prevent：动词，"预防"。

❼ dandruff：名词，"头皮屑"。

❽ sissy：形容词，"娘娘腔的"。

❾ shave：名词，"刮胡子"。

　◀ 此单词也可以当动词，意思是"刮胡子"。

❿ shampoo：名词，"洗头"。

What's next? 结果如何呢?

Robert: Would he blow-dry my hair, please?

Linda: Of course. If you want, he can even give you a facial for free.

Robert: How amazing! It just costs me NT250 dollars for a decent haircut. Hey, guys, how do I look?

Simon: The same as usual.

Robert: Come on. Give me something nice.

Linda: You're gorgeous!

罗伯特：他会把我的头发吹干吗？

琳　达：当然了。要是你要求的话，他甚至可以免费替你修脸。

罗伯特：太神奇了！才新台币两百五十元就可以拥有一个像样的发型。喂，我看起来怎么样？

西　蒙：跟平常一样。

罗伯特：别这样啦！说几句好话。

琳　达：帅呆了！

必备活用单词

❶ facial：名词，"脸部美容"。

❷ decent：形容词，"像样的"。

❸ haircut：名词，"理发"。

句型

1. S + make + O + OC

SVOOC句型就是说此句子中的宾语不完整，需要多添加词汇来修饰，而这个OC就是宾语补足语，此位置的词汇是专门用来补充说明宾语的状态。例如："I saw him crying." 中 crying 就是用来修饰him 的状态。宾语一般可以是"形容词"、"名词"，可是 make 在 SVOOC句型中，其宾语补足语还可是"动词"，不过，必须用动词原形，例如，"She makes me laugh."（她使我开怀大笑。）

2. it cost + 数量

cost本身有"花费"之意，这单词通常很少用人当主语，大多用形式主语it或物当主语。例如我们说"这本书花了我两千美元"，可写成 "This book cost me two thousand dollars. = It cost me two thousand dollars to buy this book."。

这样说最地道！

到了发廊（hair salon），该如何用英文告诉理发师自己想要的发型（hair style）呢？通常我们可以说要修剪（a trimming）、剪发（to cut hair）、烫发（to perm hair）、做造型（to set hair）、染发（to dye hair）、或最单纯的洗发（a shampoo）、旁分（to part）等等。

 这个单元的内容都记熟了吗？继续加油，准备前往下一个单元啰！

Unit 5 如何询问发型
情境英语速成会话

Unit 6
Congratulations!
如何道恭喜

Robert will attend a wedding. Wait, he is not the bridegroom.
It's for Rose's sister. For Robert, traditional Taiwanese
weddings are very interesting, so he shoots with V8 all
along the way. Let's join the wedding through Robert's
camera lens.

Robert要去参加婚礼。等等，别想太多，新郎不是他，那是Rose姐姐的婚礼（Rose是Luke的女朋友）。传统的台湾婚礼仪式实在有趣，Robert一路用V8拍摄下台湾人的结婚仪式，让我们也跟着Robert的镜头去看看这场婚礼吧！

 **现在是什么情况?**

Robert: Your sister is the prettiest bride in the world.

Rose: Thanks, Robert. She'll be very happy hearing you say that. Let's go congratulate her.

Robert: Oh, no. Don't say congratulations to the bride, but to the bridegroom.

Rose: What for?

Robert: When you say congratulations to a bride, it means you think finally someone wants her.

中文翻译

罗伯特：你姐姐是世界上最漂亮的新娘。

罗　丝：罗伯特，谢谢。听到你这么说，她一定很开心。我们去跟她说声恭喜。

罗伯特：喔，不行。不能跟新娘说恭喜，要跟新郎说。

罗　丝：为什么?

罗伯特：当你跟新娘这么说的时候，那表示你认为她好不容易找到愿意娶她的人了。

Rose: What should I say instead?

Robert: Just say "I wish you a lot of happiness."

Rose: I really hope she will be happy. You know, my mother always wants to marry her to a millionaire, but her husband isn't.

Robert: What does the bridegroom do?

Rose: He's a cook. My mother thinks it's shameful to marry her daughter to a poor cook.

Robert: Maybe one day he'll become a chef. What a good marriage needs is love, not money.

Rose: You're right. He does love my sister.

罗　丝：那我该怎么说？

罗伯特：只要说"我希望你过得幸福"就好了。

罗　丝：我真的希望她会快乐。你知道，我妈妈一直想将她嫁给百万富翁，可是她的丈夫却不是。

罗伯特：新郎是做什么的？

罗　丝：他是厨师。我妈觉得把女儿嫁给穷厨师很丢脸。

罗伯特：或许有一天他会成了主厨。婚姻需要的是爱，不是金钱。

罗　丝：你说得没错。他确实很爱我姐姐。

Unit 6 如何道恭喜
情境英语速成会话

必备活用单词

❶ bride：名词，"新娘"。

◀ 伴娘称为bridesmaid；准新娘是 bride-to-be。

❷ bridegroom：名词，"新郎"。

◀ 男傧相称为bridesman。

❸ chef：名词，"主厨"。

 ## What's next? 结果如何呢？

Robert: Rose, you're in my way.

Rose: Sorry. Robert, can you take a shot of that scene with your digital camera?

Robert: No problem. Why did your sister throw a fan out of a car window?

Rose: It means she is giving up her original last name for her husband, and using his last name.

Robert: How weird. Will you do that in your wedding?

Rose: I don't know, but it's one part of a traditional wedding.

罗伯特：罗丝，你挡住我了。

罗　丝：对不起。罗伯特，可以把那个镜头拍进数码相机里吗？

罗伯特：没问题。为什么你姐姐从车窗丢出一把扇子？

罗　丝：那表示她要为丈夫放弃原本的姓氏，改用她丈夫的。

罗伯特：好奇怪喔！你结婚的时候也会这么做吗？

罗　丝：我不知道。不过，那可是传统婚礼的一部分。

 句型

| My mother always wants to marry her to a millionaire. | 我妈一直想把她嫁给百万富翁。 |

结婚是一种动作，大多会用动词 marry 来表示，嫁娶之间不用介词 to。例如，约翰娶了玛丽为妻，英文说 "John married Mary."；玛丽嫁给约翰，则是 "Mary married John."。表示已婚的状态，只要将 marry 改成过去式即可，例如："Bill is married."（比尔已经结婚了。）

 这样说最地道！

以前有个理财广告，打的是婚礼（wedding）。在东方，婚礼是由男方主导；在西方，婚礼却是新娘的舞台。也就是说，西方人结婚时，婚礼若不是在教堂（church）举行，通常会在新娘家举行，而婚礼的开销也由女方支付。婚礼上的客人，大多会以礼物（present）当作结婚贺礼，而非礼金（a cash gift）。所以，广告中的法国人生了四个女儿，他趁早买了基金，替女儿的婚礼做好财务规划，以免到时候捉襟见肘。

Unit 7
Thanks, I'm full.
吃饱了怎么说&如何拒绝

Robert attends the wedding of Rose's sister. Chinese food is wonderful, and everything is very delicious. But… Rose's aunt, Aunty Jo, is very enthusiastic. She passes him everything. Oh, boy, how is he going to refuse her?

Robert 参加 Rose 姐姐的结婚典礼。中国菜真是太棒了，什么东西都好吃。可是 Rose 的阿姨 Aunty Jo 很热情，什么都要夹一块给他。哦，他要如何拒绝别人呢？

现在是什么情况?

Robert: It's interesting. They set the firecrackers off before the wedding breakfast.

Aunty Jo: It's just not the same without the noise. Have some five-spice watermelon seeds.

Robert: Um, it tastes not too bad. These seeds are what we're going to eat?

Aunty Jo: Of course not, young man. Look, the food's coming out. Try the steamed chicken.

Robert: Why do they serve chicken first?

Aunty Jo: It's a metaphor: Chicken in Chinese sounds like building a house.

罗伯特：很有趣。他们在喜宴前放鞭炮。

阿　姨：没有这些响声，气氛就不一样了。来，尝尝五香瓜子。

罗伯特：嗯，还不错。这些瓜子就是我们要吃的东西吗？

阿　姨：年轻人，当然不是。看，菜来了。尝尝这道蒸鸡。

罗伯特：为什么先上鸡肉？

阿　姨：这是个隐喻：中文里头，鸡的发音跟成家是同一个音。

Robert: What's that? It looks like a roll of paper.

Aunty Jo: It's called Fried Spring Roll. Have one. It's very crispy.

Robert: (He takes a bite.) You're right.

Aunty Jo: Have more. There is plenty of them.

Robert: No, thanks. I'm full.

罗伯特：那是什么？看起来好像一卷纸。

阿　姨：那叫炸春卷。吃一个看看。非常酥脆喔！

罗伯特：（他咬了一口）没错。

阿　姨：多吃几个。还很多。

罗伯特：不，谢了。我已经饱了。

 必备活用单词

❶ firecracker：名词，"鞭炮"。

❷ wedding breakfast：名词，"喜宴"。

❸ spice：名词，"香料"。

❹ metaphor：名词，"隐喻"。

Unit 7 吃饱了怎么说 & 如何拒绝
情境英语速成会话

❺ roll：名词，"卷"。

❻ Fried Spring Roll：名词，"春卷"。

❼ crispy：形容词，"酥脆的"。

❽ bite：动词，"咬"。

What's next? 结果如何呢？

Aunty Jo: Fried bitter melon. On such a hot day, you should try this.

Robert:　(He spits it out) Aunty Jo. I can't eat this! It's too bitter.

Aunty Jo: Don't worry. Just leave it. How about the loach herb soup? It's very good for men.

Robert:　Loach? Give me a break, Aunty Jo.

Aunty Jo: Don't you want yourself to be a sexy and powerful young man?

Robert:　Not this time, thanks.

阿　姨：炸苦瓜。这么热的天气，你该尝尝这个。

罗伯特：（他吐了出来）阿姨。我没办法吃下去。这太苦了。

阿　姨：别担心。放着吧！那来点中药泥鳅汤，如何？那对男人可是有很大的好处。

罗伯特：泥鳅？饶了我吧，阿姨。

阿　姨：年轻人，难道你不想自己变得性感又强壮吗？

罗伯特：谢了，下次吧！

句型

| It's just not the same without the noise. | 没有这些声响，气氛就不一样了。 |

我们先来看看语法的部分，首先，两个否定词在一起（not和 without），所以是负负得正，变成 "it's just the same with the noise."。很有趣吧？至于用法，这句的用法很广，只要缺乏某样东西，气氛就会变得不一样，都可以透过这句话来表达那种意思。

这样说最地道！

英文里头有许多话语是跟吃有关的，例如: You can't have your cake and eat it. (鱼与熊掌不能兼得。)；The proof of the pudding is in the eating. (不吃布丁，不知其味) 意思就是说 "凡事要亲身体验，才能真正了解"，这句话跟 "如人饮水，冷暖自知" 非常相似；Hunger is the best sauce. (饥饿是最好的调味料。)，也就是说肚子饿的时候，什么东西都是山珍海味。

Unit 8
Let's have a baby shower.
如何选购礼物

Peter, a father-to-be, is Luke's colleague, and his wife Lisa is pregnant and is due next month. Robert will have an excellent baby shower for Peter's wife. It might make Peter feel relieved.

Luke 的同事 Peter 要当爸爸了。他的太太 Lisa 怀孕已八个月，下个月要生了。Robert 计划替 Peter 的老婆举办一个别开生面的送礼派对，让这位准爸爸好好放松一下心情。

现在是什么情况?

Robert: Lisa's due in four weeks, so I want to have a baby shower for her.

Rose: That's a good idea. Wait, a baby shower? Is that a kind of party?

Robert: Definitely. We usually have a shower a month or two before the baby's arrival.

Rose: Here, we celebrate with red eggs and presents until they are born a month later. Why have the party before the babies come?

Robert: You got me. Maybe the mother-to-be knows what she needs to buy after getting gifts.

Rose: I see. How about some diapers and stick-ons for the baby?

罗伯特：丽萨再过四周就要生了，所以我想替她举行一个送礼派对。

罗　丝：好主意。等等，送礼派对？那是派对吗？

罗伯特：当然。我们通常在小孩出生的前一、两个月举行送礼派对。

罗　丝：在台湾，直到小孩出生了一个月后，我们才以红蛋和礼物作为庆祝。为什么在孩子落地前送礼呢？

罗伯特：这可把我问倒了。或许，拿到礼物后，准妈妈就会知道自己该准备哪些东西。

罗　丝：我懂了。那给小宝宝买些尿片和黏贴玩具如何？

(All of Peter's friends get together in his house. Luke's late for the party and he's going to say "Hi" to Lisa.)

Lisa:　Oww. Ooh-OUCH!

Luke:　What's wrong with you, Lisa?

Lisa:　The little fat boy kicked at me.

Luke:　That doesn't sound too good. Lisa, how is your pregnancy?

Lisa:　Terrible, you know, morning sickness, stomachache, contractions and so on.

Luke:　I'm glad I'm not a woman.

（彼得所有朋友全聚在一块。卢克迟到了，正要跟丽萨打招呼。）

丽　萨：喔。唉唷！

卢　克：丽萨，你怎么了？

丽　萨：肚子里的小胖弟刚踢了我一下。

卢　克：你听起来不太妙。丽萨，你在怀孕期间还好吧？

丽　萨：太糟了，孕吐、肚子痛还有子宫收缩等等。

卢　克：我很庆幸我不是女人。

Unit 8 如何选购礼物
情境英语速成会话

必备活用单词

❶ due：形容词，"到期的"。

◀ 此处的 due 指的是产期；当然，任何东西到期了，如图书馆的借书，也是用 due 这个单词。

❷ baby shower：名词，"送礼派对"。

◀ 有点类似中国的满月，不同的是，参加送礼派对的亲朋好友，是送些婴儿可能用到的日常用品，而非黄金、首饰等贵重金属。

❸ celebrate：动词，"庆祝"。

❹ mother-to-be：名词，"准妈妈"。

❺ diaper：名词，"尿布"。

❻ stick-on：名词，"黏贴小物品"。

◀ 这类小物品都是背后有吸盘、黏胶的小东西。

❼ morning sick：名词，"孕吐"。

❽ contraction：名词，"收缩"。

◀ 子宫收缩。

What's next? 结果如何呢?

Robert: You look close.

Lisa: I am. I'm due next month, maybe earlier.

Robert: I brought some baby clothes and toys for you. I hope you like my presents.

Lisa: They're very lovely. I've been looking for a Teddy Bear like this for my baby.

Robert: I bought them on the Internet. These are from Rose.

Lisa: Wow, two boxes of diapers and bottles!

Robert: She supposed that the baby will need them all the time.

罗伯特：你好像快生了。

丽　萨：是啊！我下个月就要生了，可能更早一点。

罗伯特：我带了些婴儿衣服和玩具给你。希望你会喜欢我送的礼物。

丽　萨：好可爱喔！我一直在替宝宝找像这样的泰迪熊。

罗伯特：我在网站上买的。这些是罗丝送的。

丽　萨：哇，两大盒的尿布和奶瓶。

罗伯特：她想小孩总是需要这些东西。

Unit 8 如何选购礼物
情境英语速成会话

句型

1. You got me.　　　你考倒我了。

用来表示对方的问题考倒了自己，可用"You got me."。而"I get (got) it."是"我懂了、我知道了"之意，可别把这两个搞错了。

2. What's wrong with + 人？　　（某人）怎么了？

询问别人的身体、情形出了什么状况，可以用"What's wrong with you?"；此外，此句也有"褒义"，如别人老是出错，用来质问对方到底怎么了，也可用"What's wrong with you?"。而"What's up? / What's the matter?"也有"怎么了"之意。

这样说最地道！

通常女孩想知道自己是否怀孕（pregnancy），通常会到超市买一下验孕试剂（pregnancy test）来测验看看。若是怀孕了，接踵而来的就是一些避免不了的身体反应，如孕吐（morning sick）、尿频（micturition）、肚子痛（stomachache）、恶心（nausea）等等。到了要生产（go into labor）的阶段了，子宫（womb）便开始收缩（contraction），这一连串的苦难，让人觉得母亲真伟大。

Unit 8 如何选购礼物
情境英语速成会话

Unit 9
I'm sorry for your loss.
吊唁＆安慰

Simon's father passed away. Linda had the same experience as Simon did, so she can understand how Simon feels. She encourages Simon to look on the bright side. Let's see the touching scene.

Simon 的父亲过世了。同样也有丧父之痛的 Linda，
鼓励 Simon 要坚强。我们来看看这感人的一幕。

现在是什么情况？

Linda: Simon's father passed away yesterday.

Robert: I'm really sorry to hear that. How did it happen?

Linda: A heart attack. He was having dinner with his wife to celebrate their wedding anniversary.

Robert: When is his father's funeral?

Linda: This Friday. To attend a funeral, he will leave for Germany this afternoon.

Robert: Let's go to his place. Maybe he needs someone to help him pack.

· ·

中文翻译

琳　达：西蒙的父亲昨天去世了。

罗伯特：听到这消息，真是令人难过。怎么发生的？

琳　达：心脏病。他正跟太太用餐，庆祝结婚周年纪念日。

罗伯特：他父亲的丧礼何时举行？

琳　达：这个周五。为了参加丧礼，他今天下午要前往德国了。

罗伯特：走，到他的住处。或许他需要别人来帮他打包行李。

(They're in Simon's apartment. He's weeping.)

Linda: Is there anything Robert and I can do for you?

Simon: I don't want to put you out.

Linda: You look exhausted. Simon, you really need a break.

Simon: I can't. If I had listened to him and stayed home with him, such an accident would not have happened.

Linda: It's not your fault. It happens.

Robert: She's right. Don't take it too seriously.

（他们在西蒙的公寓。他正在哭泣。）

琳　达：我和罗伯特有什么可帮得上忙的吗？

西　蒙：我不想给你们添麻烦。

琳　达：你看起来很疲倦。西蒙，你得休息一下。

西　蒙：我没办法。要是我听他的话，留在家里陪他，这样的意外也不会发生了。

琳　达：那不是你的错。这是无法避免的。

罗伯特：她说得没错。别把这件事看得太重。

Unit 9 吊唁＆安慰
情境英语速成会话

必备活用单词

❶ pass away：动词词组，"过世"。

◀ 有关死亡的用法很多，最直接的用法是用 die；报纸杂志的用法则是 perish，而 pass away 和 pass on 是最婉转的用法。

❷ heart attack：名词，"心脏病"。

◀ have a heart attach是"有心脏病"之意。表示有了病痛的动词，用have即可。

❸ wedding anniversary：名词，"结婚周年纪念日"。

◀ wedding是"婚礼"之意；anniversary则是"纪念日"之意。

❹ funeral：名词，"丧礼"。

◀ 丧礼可以在殡仪馆（funeral home）或教堂举行。信教者大多在教堂举行，因为丧礼上有牧师帮死者作简单的生平介绍，然后在圣歌和圣诗中结束，感觉非常祥和安宁。

❺ leave for：动词词组，"前往"。

❻ pack：动词，"打包"。

❼ weep：动词，"哭泣"。

❽ exhausted：形容词，"疲倦的"。

9 break：名词，"休息"。

◀ take a break 就是"休息片刻"。

What's next? 结果如何呢?

Linda: I'm sorry for your loss. It must be tough for you.

Simon: I don't know what I would do without your help.

Linda: Never mind. A friend in need is a friend indeed.

Simon: He was a good father. He was always there for me when I needed support.

Linda: I know how you feel. He will be missed.

Simon: I feel much better. Thanks for coming.

中文
翻译

琳达：你失去家人，我感到很难过。对你来说一定很难熬。

西蒙：要不是你来帮忙，我真不知该怎么办。

琳达：别放在心上。患难见真情。

西蒙：他是个好父亲。他总是在我有困难之际，伸出援手。

琳达：我了解你的感受。大家会想念他的。

西蒙：我觉得好多了。谢谢你来。

 句型

1. I'm really sorry ...　　　为某事感到抱歉、难过

sorry有"难过、抱歉、感伤"之意，视情况来决定其中文翻译。sorry之后可接不定词to，然后跟上动词原形；或加上that后面跟着从句也可以。"sorry for + 人"除了可表示"为某人感到难过、伤感"外，尚表示"替某人感到可悲"。例如："I'm sorry to heart the bad news."（听到这坏消息，我感到好难过。）；"You did such a bad thing, and I feel sorry for you."（你做了如此糟糕的坏事，我替你感到可悲。）。

2. to put someone out　　　麻烦某人

当我们不想麻烦某人时，可以说"I don't want to put you out."。这句话是跟"I'm sorry to bother you."(麻烦你，我觉得很抱歉。)一样，都是应酬话。不过，"I don't want to put you out."是真的不想麻烦别人的话；"I'm sorry to bother you."则是在准备打扰别人之前所说的场面话。这样懂了吗？

这样说最地道！

人生自古谁无死，西方国家，人死了之后第一件事就是跟医生申请死亡证明（a death certificate），再向警察局或户政事务所报备，并领取埋葬证明书，整个丧礼才可以进行。从死亡到下葬，有几道海内外皆同的程序：穿丧服（to put on mourning）、将尸体放入棺木（to coffin）、埋葬（to burry）。死者的家属得替死者披麻戴孝（wear armband）；亲朋好友则可参加丧礼（attend a funeral）、献上花圈（send a wreath）来表达对死者的纪念。

 这个单元的内容都记熟了吗？继续加油，准备前往下一个单元啰！

Unit 10
What do you think I should bring with me?
询问意见&表示认同

Rose had a car accident, and one of her legs was broken. She was hospitalized. Robert wants to visit the sick, but he doesn't know what he should bring with him. He doesn't want to go there empty-handed. So, he asks his classmate, Linda, for advice. Do you know what Robert will bring with him?

Rose 不幸发生交通意外，跌断了一条腿，住进了医院。Robert 想到医院探望她，却不知该准备什么慰问礼？他可不想当"五根香蕉一族"。所以，他向同学 Linda 请教一番。你知道 Robert 最后带了什么东西到医院吗？

现在是什么情况?

Robert: My roommate's girlfriend had a car accident. She is hospitalized.

Linda: I'm sorry to hear about that.

Robert: I'll visit the sick this afternoon. What do you think I should bring with me? You know, I don't want to go empty-handed and embarrass her.

Linda: How about flowers? They're good for everyone.

Robert: She's allergic to pollen. Besides, she's very important to me.

罗伯特：我室友的女友出了车祸。她现在正在住院。

琳　达：我听了好难过。

罗伯特：我今天下午会去探病。你想我该随身带什么礼物？你知道，我不想空手而去，使她觉得尴尬。

琳　达：送花如何？花适合送给每个人。

罗伯特：她对花粉过敏。还有，她可是重要人物。

Linda: What's wrong with her?

Robert: She has a bone fracture as well as nausea.

Linda: Can she eat normally?

Robert: No. Why do you ask?

Linda: Bottles of calcium or chicken broth are good for her.

Robert: I couldn't agree with you more.

琳　达：她有哪些病征？

罗伯特：她骨折和恶心。

琳　达：那她可以正常进食吗？

罗伯特：不。为什么问这个？

琳　达：几瓶钙片或鸡汤对她挺不错的。

罗伯特：你说得一点也没错。

 ## 必备活用单词

❶ car accident：名词，"车祸"。

◀ accident 和 incident是两个非常常见的单词，前者指的是"意外事故"，后者是"偶发的意外事件"。

❷ hospitalize：动词，"住院"。

◀ 住院的名词是"hospitalization"，形容词是"hospitalized"。若以词组形式表示，则为"be in hospital"。

❸ visit the sick：动词词组，"探病"。

　　◀ the sick 是由 the + 形容词所形成的名词，代表"病人"。

❹ empty-handed：形容词，"空手"。

　　◀ 此单词亦可当副词。

❺ embarrass：动词，"使局促不安、尴尬"。

❻ allergic：形容词，"过敏"。

　　◀ 对某物品过敏为 be allergic to + 物品。

❼ pollen：名词，"花粉"。

　　◀ 此为不可数名词。

❽ besides：副词，"还有、此外"。

❾ syndrome：名词，"症状"。

❿ fracture：名词，"破碎"。

　　◀ 骨折的英文为 a fracture of the bone。

⓫ normally：副词，"正常地"。

⓬ calcium：名词，"钙"。

⓭ broth：名词，"肉汤"。

◀ chicken broth是"鸡汤"之意。西方人生病时，不像中国人如此依赖药材进补，所以他们最好的进补食物是一锅鸡汤，跟中国人喝人参鸡汤是同样的道理。探病时，熟识的朋友也会带来鸡汤聊表心意。

What's next? 结果如何呢?

Linda:　How is Rose doing?

Robert:　She's getting better and better. Thanks. Your chicken broth and calcium did a good job. She liked them very much. How did you exactly know what she needed?

Linda:　A female's sixth sense.

Robert:　Not funny.

Linda:　Robert, you're not as thoughtful as I am at all. First, she has a broken leg, so calcium is best for her bones; second, she had nausea, and it meant that she must have lost her appetite. Liquid food might be her first choice.

Robert:　Wow, you're terrific.

琳　达：罗丝最近还好吧?

罗伯特：逐渐康复中。多谢。你建议的鸡汤和钙片帮了大忙。她很喜欢这两样东西。你怎么知道她要什么?

琳　达：全靠女人的第六感。

罗伯特：不好笑。

Unit 10 询问意见&表示认同
情境英语速成会话

琳　达：罗伯特，你一点也不像我那么体贴。首先，她腿断了，钙片有益于她的骨头；第二，她感到恶心，那表示她肯定胃口全失。液体食物是她的最佳选择。

罗伯特：哇，你太厉害了。

 必备活用单词

❶ exactly：副词，"确切"。

❷ female：名词，"女性"。

❸ sixth sense：名词，"第六感"。

❹ thoughtful：形容词，"体贴、替人着想的"。

❺ appetite：名词，"胃口"。

❻ liquid：形容词，"液体的"。

❼ terrific：形容词，"太棒了、太厉害了"。

 句型

1. Do you think...　你认为……

询问别人意见之际，我们可以用以上的句型，然后在 think 后面接上一个句子；或是 "How do you think it is a good idea to ..."。例如："How do you think it's a good idea to bring him flowers?"（你觉得把花送他好吗？）。

2. I couldn't agree with you more　你说得太对了

表示同意别人的意见、话语，最常听到的是 "You're right."、"You got the right point." 或 "I can't agree with you more."。此外，"You can say it twice." 或 "You can say it again."，也是表示非常同意他人的惯用句子。

 这样说最地道！

一般来说，美国的大医院不看门诊，小病可以先打电话给自己的家庭医生（family doctor），然后自行到超市（supermarket）买成药（patent medicine），要是病痛严重一些，才找上开业医生（physician's office）、小诊所（clinic）。在美国，好像做什么都得预约（appointment），连看医生也一样。

Unit 11
What about a blind date?
如何当红娘 & 如何介绍双方

Chinese Valentine's Day is coming. There are couples holding hands together all over the streets. When the scene comes to him, he feels so lonely. Because Rose and Luke are so intimate at home, Robert feels that he is isolated. Rose senses his loneliness. She decides to arrange a match for him. Do you know whom Robert will fall in love with?

七夕情人节到了，Robert 见到街上到处是情人，有感而发。回到家，Rose 和 Luke又亲亲热热，他顿时觉得好寂寞。善解人意的 Rose 看出他的寂寞，替他安排了一场相亲大会。你知道最后 Robert 会情归何处吗？

现在是什么情况？

(Today is Valentine's Day. In the morning a delivery boy comes and hands Robert a basket of roses.)

Rose: Wow! What a huge basket of roses.

Robert: This just came for you. Who's this Mr. Secret Admirer?

Rose: Luke. (She reads the card with the flowers.)

Robert: What's the matter? You've gotten that look.

Rose: What look?

Robert: Like you're in seventh heaven, on cloud nine...

（今天是情人节。一大早快递小弟便交给罗伯特一大篮的玫瑰花。）

罗　丝：哇！好大的一篮玫瑰。

罗伯特：这刚送到，给你的。谁是这位神秘的仰慕者啊？

罗　丝：（她阅读附于花上的卡片）卢克。

罗伯特：怎么了？你那是什么表情。

罗　丝：什么表情？

罗伯特：快乐似神仙的表情。

Rose: Luke wants to propose to me. Look at this sweetheart ring hidden among the roses.

Robert: This guy means business?

Rose: What do you mean?

Robert: You've known each other less than two years. Do you think he is your Mr. Right?

Rose: OF COURSE. He's the only one in the world I want to spend the rest of my life with.

Robert: Congratulations! Your Mr. Right is behind you.

罗　　丝：卢克想跟我求婚。快看这藏在玫瑰花里头的情人对戒。

罗伯特：这家伙当真吗？

罗　　丝：你的意思是什么？

罗伯特：你们两个认识不到两年。你觉得他是你的白马王子吗？

罗　　丝：当然了。他可是这世界上我愿意一起共度后半辈子的人。

罗伯特：恭喜了！你的白马王子就站在后头。

必备活用单词

❶ blind date：名词，"盲目约会"。

◀ 请别误会，blind date 并非是两人约会都很盲目，或根本搞不清状况的意思。blind date 的意思是指约会的男女两人根本不曾碰面，也不认识对方，只凭朋友的介绍便来见对方一面。这样什么都不知道的约会，不是跟"blind"一样吗？

❷ Valentine's Day：名词，"情人节"。

❸ delivery boy：名词，"快递小弟"。

◀ delivery本身是名词，动词是deliver。

❹ Mr. Secret Admirer：名词，"神秘仰慕者"。

◀ secret是"神秘的"之意；admirer是"仰慕者"之意。英文中，很喜欢将Mr. / Miss和一些名词搭配使用，感觉比较活泼生动。

❺ propose：动词，"求婚"。

◀ 求婚的名词为proposal；propose还有"计划、提议"之意。

❻ sweetheart ring：名词，"情人对戒"。

❼ Mr. Right：名词，"白马王子"。

❽ congratulations：名词，"恭喜"。

◀ 英文的恭喜大多用复数，动词为congratulate。

 What's next? 结果如何呢？

(After dinner, Robert, Rose and Luke are in the living room. Luke and Rose are discussing their arrangement of their proposal wedding.)

Rose: Why are you so glum?

Robert: I'm really happy for you two, but I'm really very lonely.

Rose: I'm sorry for neglecting you.

Robert: No, I don't mean that. Look at you, you're so happy. I need a girlfriend who can keep me company, share my happiness and sadness, and listen to my sweet talk.

Rose: My friend, Jessica, is single. I think you are two of a kind. But she's Miss Particular.

Robert: Why don't you introduce her to me, and then see what might happen?

（晚饭后，罗伯特、罗丝和卢克来到客厅。卢克和罗丝正在讨论如何安排他们的订婚典礼。）

罗　丝：你怎么闷闷不乐？

罗伯特：我很替你们两个高兴，可是我挺寂寞的。

罗　丝：对不起忽略了你。

罗伯特：不，我不是那个意思。看看你们两个好开心的样子，我也想要一个女朋友，可以陪伴我，分享我的喜悦和悲伤，还可以听听我的甜言蜜语。

罗　丝：我的好朋友杰茜卡还是单身。我想你们两人很般配。不过，她可是位挑剔小姐。

罗伯特：何不把她介绍给我，然后看看后续发展？

必备活用单词

❶ arrangement：名词，"安排"。

　　◀ 动词形式为arrange。

❷ glum：形容词，"闷闷不乐的"。

　　◀ Why are you so glum?用来询问对方为何看起来如此不快乐，或是对方臭脸的时候，都可以派上用场。

❸ neglect：动词，"忽视、忽略"。

❹ company：动词，"陪伴"。

❺ sweet talk：名词，"甜言蜜语、花言巧语"。

　　◀ 此处 Robert 用 sweet talk 来表示他现在连说花言巧语都没人听了。英文口语中，表示"绵绵的情话"是 sweet nothings。

❻ two of a kind："个性相似"。

❼ Miss Particular：名词，"挑剔小姐"。

　　◀ particular有"特殊的、详细的、讲究的"之意。

句型

1. You've gotten that look.	你那是什么表情。

当我们看见别人脸色大变，不管是变好，还是变坏，我们都可用"You've gotten that look."，用来询问别人现在的心情，要不，怎么会有那样的"变脸效应"呢？若是说者有意，听者无心，那么，听者可以回一句"What look?"（什么表情？），作为搪塞。

2. You're in the seventh heaven, on cloud nine.	你快乐似神仙。

表示处于极端快乐，仿佛跟神仙一样的境界，可以用"Someone's in the seventh heaven, on cloud nine."这句话。中文不是有句"九层云霄"，就是这意思了。

这样说最地道！

碰上节庆，人家说孤家寡人（single）最可怜了。他们只要一出门，就是满山满谷的情侣（couples），手牵着手，或是穿上情人装，卿卿我我，无视他人的存在，简直是情人眼中出西施（Love is blind）。这在单身汉（bachelor）或老小姐（spinster）看来，简直有点伤风败俗。说到这，让人不禁怀疑到底是什么原因造成有人形影孤单？是个性不合而造成分手（to break up）、被甩（be dumped），还是有人脚踏两条船（to two-time）呢？

Unit 12
Are you free tonight?
如何约她出来&
如何展开约会话题

When Robert first sees Jessica, he thinks she is the woman he has been looking for. But he is told that Jessica is very conservative. How will he make a pass at her? Is it OK to have the first date in a café? Please pray for Robert whether you're single or not.

Robert 第一眼看到 Jessica 就喜欢上她，认为眼前的她就是他今生的新娘。可是，听说 Jessica 很保守，他该怎么展开攻势？第一次约会在咖啡馆好不好呢？不管你单身与否，请替可怜的 Robert 祷告吧！

现在是什么情况?

(Linda and Robert are in the student cafeteria.)

Linda: What's wrong with you? You're absent-minded.

Robert: I think I'm falling in love.

Linda: Really? Who's the lucky girl?

Robert: You don't know her. She's a friend of a friend. We met on a blind date. When I first saw her, I knew she was the girl I had been looking for.

（琳达和罗伯特在学生餐厅。）

琳　达：你怎么了？心不在焉的。

罗伯特：我想我恋爱了。

琳　达：真的？谁是那个幸运儿？

罗伯特：你不认识她。她是我朋友的朋友。我们在配对约会中认识的。我第一眼看见她，我就知道她是我想要的女人。

Linda: Did you try to make a pass at her?

Robert: I do want to try, but I don't know how to make a good start.

Linda: Poor guy. What're you afraid of?

Robert: Everything. If I ask her for a date, I might strike out. Do you think I have another chance to win her back?

Linda: You worry too much. How was her first impression of you?

Robert: I don't know. I'm too chicken to know the truth.

Linda: You are off on the wrong foot.

Robert: What do you mean?

Linda: Ask her out. You've got nothing to lose.

琳　达：你试着对她展开攻势了吗？

罗伯特：我也想去试啊！可是，我不知道该如何开始。

琳　达：可怜的家伙。你在怕什么？

罗伯特：一切。要是我约她出去，被她给三振出局。你想，我还有其他的机会赢回来吗？

琳　达：你担心太多了。她对你的第一印象如何？

罗伯特：我不知道。我太胆小了，不敢知道真相。

琳　达：你打从开头就做错了。

罗伯特：什么意思？

琳　达：把她约出来。你不会有什么损失的。

必备活用单词

❶ cafeteria：名词，"自助餐厅"。

◀ 这类的自助餐跟中国的自助餐厅很像，顾客得自己动手，到一排排的食物区拿菜，然后去结账。

❷ absent-minded：形容词，"心不在焉的"。

❸ make a pass at ... ：动词词组，"展开攻势"。

◀ 表示对某人展开攻势，只要在介词at之后接上某人即可。

❹ strike out：动词词组，"删除"。

❺ impression：名词，"印象"。

◀ 表示对某事物有好印象，得用主语 + have a good impression on + 宾语。

❻ ask one out：动词词组，"约某人出去"。

What's next? 结果如何呢？

(Robert picks up the phone.)

Robert:　Hi, this is Robert. May I speak to Jessica?

Jessica:　Speaking.

Robert:　I got two concert tickets. I don't know if you're free tomorrow night.

Jessica: Well, it's hard to say.

Robert: (He waits for a few seconds and sighs.) I want to get it straight. I'm dying to see you after I met you last week, but… all right. I am ready for the worst.

Jessica: (She laughs.) How about tomorrow lunch time? I might leave for Hong Kong for a business trip at 5:00 p.m.

（罗伯特拿起话筒。）

罗伯特：嗨，我是罗伯特。请问杰茜卡在吗?

杰茜卡：我就是。

罗伯特：我有两张音乐会的票。不知道你明晚有没有空?

杰茜卡：嗯，很难说耶。

罗伯特：（他等了几秒钟，叹口气）我想要把话说清楚。自从上周跟你碰面，我就很想见你，可是……好吧，我已经有最坏的打算了。

杰茜卡：（她笑了）明天午餐时间如何? 我下午五点可能得前往香港出差。

Unit 12 如何约她出来&如何展开约会话题
情境英语速成会话

句型

1. get nothing to lose	没什么好损失

这句话通常可用来鼓励别人勇往直前，做事不要老是畏畏缩缩、怕东怕西的。

2. be ready for the worst	做好万全准备

"已经替最糟糕的做好准备"，有点类似中文的做了最坏的打算，如果再坏，也没什么好担心害怕的了。

3. for a business trip	出差

"出差"除了可用"go to + 地点 + for a business trip"，动词也可改成"have a business trip"。

这样说最地道！

想要找到真爱（true love），有时候比中彩票（lottery）还要难。不过，还是有几个好方法：扩展自己的社交生活（social life），请亲朋好友大力推销，还可参加婚友联谊（love feast）这类认识单身男女指数高的活动。寻觅爱人的开头，总是跟漏网捕鱼一样，可能是一网多鱼，所以，交朋友过程中尽量不要产生三角习题（love triangle），要不然，成了猎艳高手（lady-killer），自己的评比指数可能很低喔！

Unit 13
You are really something.
表达欣赏之意

At last, Robert asked Jessica out. He is so happy. They went to Shihlin Night Market, and ate some delicious food. Oh, no. After he walked Jessica home, he found out he got lost. What should Robert do to solve the problem?

好不容易把 Jessica 约出来了，Robert 乐得仿佛
飞上了天。他们逛了士林夜市，吃了不少东西。可
是，麻烦来了——当他送 Jessica 回家后，却发现
自己迷路了，Robert 该怎么办呢？

现在是什么情况?

(Robert takes Jessica to an expensive restaurant.)

Jessica: It's too expensive to eat here.

Robert: I thought a beautiful lady like you likes such a luxurious restaurant.

Jessica: Some do. But I'm not one of them. I prefer eating in the night market. Listen, I'm not into appearances.

Robert: You're something.

Jessica: Have you ever been to Shihlin night market?

Robert: No. Want to be my tour guide?

（罗伯特带杰茜卡到一家高级餐厅。）

杰茜卡：在这里吃饭太贵了。

罗伯特：我想像你这样漂亮的淑女，会喜欢高级餐厅。

杰茜卡：有些人确实喜欢。可是我不是其中之一。我比较倾向到夜市吃东西。听着，那跟外表没关系。

罗伯特：你真的很了不起。

杰茜卡：你去过士林夜市吗?

罗伯特：没有。要不要当我的向导呢?

(They find a stand and order something to eat.)

Robert: Are you seeing anyone now?

Jessica: I suppose not.

Robert: Well, I know it's very straight forward, but what do you think of me? I'm really crazy for you.

Jessica: You're gentle, serious, and humorous. But I don't want to get serious yet.

Robert: Because I'm not your type?

Jessica: Of course not. I just need some more time to know who you are.

（他们找到摊位，点些东西来吃。）

罗伯特：你现在正和别人交往吗？

杰茜卡：应该没有。

罗伯特：我知道那有些直接，不过，你觉得我这个人怎样？我真的很喜欢你。

杰茜卡：你很绅士有礼、认真、幽默。可是，我目前不想那么认真。

罗伯特：因为我不是你喜欢的类型？

杰茜卡：不是啦！我只是需要点时间更深入了解你。

必备活用单词

❶ luxurious: 形容词，"奢华的、高级的"。

◀ "奢侈品"叫做 luxury。此外，luxury 也有"享乐、奢华"之意。

❷ prefer: 动词，"偏爱"。

◀ prefer 若后面接动词，必须用动名词 V-ing 的型态。若说"比较偏爱A而不喜欢B"的句型，可用I prefer watching TV than going shopping.。

❸ night market: 名词，"夜市"。

❹ appearance: 名词，"外表"。

◀ 说某人长得很好看，可以用形容词 good-looking 或名词 good looks 来表示。

❺ tour guide: 名词，"导游"。

◀ tour 一般意为旅游、参观；而"包团旅游"称为 package tour。

❻ stand: 名词，"摊贩"。

◀ 街上的小贩称为 street vendor。

❼ order: 动词，"订购、点菜"。

❽ suppose: 动词，"应该"。

◀ be supposed to 为"应该、可以"之意。

⑨ humorous：形容词，"幽默感的"。

◀ 幽默的名词为 humor。

⑩ type：名词，"类型、样式"。

◀ 英文中有许多类型、风格的字眼，用来指人的"类型"，应该用 type，如：She's my type.（她是我喜欢的类型。）若指事情的风格，则用 style，如 Wearing heavy makeup is not my style.（化浓妆不是我的风格。）

 What's next? 结果如何呢？

(On his way home, Robert lost way, so he called Jessica to ask the right directions.)

Robert:　I'm sorry to have bothered you again, but I got lost.

Jessica:　Do you know where you are?

Robert:　I can't find the street name, but there is a church at the corner, and a swimming pool on my right side.

Jessica:　OK, I know where you are. Can you stay there for a while until I come? It's not far away from my place.

Robert:　Jessica, I don't know how to thank you.

Jessica:　Don't mention it. I had a happy time tonight. It's my turn to do something for you.

中文
翻译

（回家途中，罗伯特迷路了，所以他打电话给杰茜卡问路。）

罗伯特：很抱歉再次打扰你，可是我迷路了。

Unit 13 表达欣赏之意
情境英语速成会话

杰茜卡：你知道自己在什么地方吗？

罗伯特：我找不到街道名称，可是街角有教堂，我的右手边是游泳池。

杰茜卡：好，我知道你人在哪里了。你可以待在原地直到我来吗？那离我住的地方不远。

罗伯特：杰茜卡，我不知道该怎么谢你。

杰茜卡：别放在心上。我今晚玩得很开心，轮到我来回报你了。

 句型

I'm sorry to have bothered you.	很抱歉打扰你了。

光看翻译，许多人容易将此句和"I'm sorry to bother you."搞混了，看起来好像都一样。其实，两者还是有很大的差别。首先，我们在打扰别人之前，会先来一段客套话，这客套话就是"I'm sorry to bother you."。等我们麻烦完别人后，准备离开时，就会说"I'm sorry to have bothered you."。从have + p.p.（现在完成式）看来，可见已经打扰过别人了。这样，是不是比较容易了解了呢？

这样说最地道！

人家说恋爱的滋味跟吃到柠檬的感觉一样，真是爱在心底口难开。其实，喜欢一个人，应该勇敢说出来。以下是恋爱时可模仿的经典名句：

You're the most beautiful woman I've ever seen.
（你是我见过最美的女人了。）

I'm crazy about you.（我为你着迷。）

You make me happy.（你让我幸福快乐。）

You're sweet.（你好漂亮。）

I want to know all about you.（我想知道你的点点滴滴。）

I think of you day and night.（我整天都在想你。）

这个单元的内容都记熟了吗？继续加油，准备前往下一个单元啰！

Unit 14
Will you marry me?
如何开口套牢她

After their relationship is steady, Robert thinks it's time for him to settle down. So, he proposed to Jessica, and she said, "YES." Now they're going to pick out their wedding rings.

交往一阵子，Robert 觉得自己也该定下来了。所以
他跟 Jessica 求婚，她也欣然同意了。现在，他们
甜蜜的小两口正要去买结婚戒指。

现在是什么情况?

(Rose, Luke and Robert are in the living room.)

Rose: What're you two going to do to kill time tonight?

Robert: We're going to see a movie.

Rose: Can Luke and I go with you?

Robert: Two's a company; three's a crowd.

Luke: Rose, don't be a third wheel. Robert has something to do tonight. (He points at his finger.)

Rose: Really? You're a well-matched couple.

· ·

中文翻译

（罗丝、卢克和罗伯特在客厅。）

罗　丝：你们两人今晚要上哪儿消磨时间?

罗伯特：我们要去看电影。

罗　丝：卢克和我可以跟吗?

罗伯特：两人恰恰好，三人嫌太挤。

卢　克：罗丝，别当电灯泡。罗伯特今晚有事得忙。（他指着自己的手指。）

罗　丝：真的吗? 你们真是天造地设的一对。

(After movie, Robert takes Jessica to a quiet café.)

Jessica: What's on your mind? You look very serious.

Robert: Do you love me?

Jessica: Of course, I love you. Do you doubt me?

Robert: Then, will you marry me?

Jessica: (Shocked.) I don't mean to pour cold water on your proposal, but are you serious?

Robert: I want you to know that I can't live without you. I've never felt like this before.

（看完电影，罗伯特带杰茜卡到一家安静的咖啡馆）

杰茜卡：你心底在想些什么？你看起来好严肃。

罗伯特：你爱我吗？

杰茜卡：当然，我爱你。你怀疑吗？

罗伯特：那，嫁给我好吗？

杰茜卡：（惊讶）我不是想泼你冷水，可是，你是认真的吗？

罗伯特：我要你知道，没有你我活不下去。我从没有过这样的感觉。

Unit 14 如何开口套牢她
情境英语速成会话

必备活用单词

❶ kill time：动词，"消磨时间"。

　　◀ 杀价可不是用 kill price 喔，而是 bargain，别搞错了。

❷ Two's a company, three's a crowd："两人恰恰好，三人嫌太挤"。

　　◀ 这句话是用来对付那些电灯泡的名言，赶紧学起来。

❸ third wheel：名词，"电灯泡"。

　　◀ 除了 two's a company, three's a crowd、third wheel，另一个电灯泡的用法是 pest；其实，pest 的原义为害虫、讨厌鬼，试想，约会时在一旁干扰的讨厌鬼不就是电灯泡了吗？这样，就比较容易记起来了。

❹ point：动词，"指着"。

　　◀ point at 为指着特定的地方。

❺ well-matched：形容词，"登对的、相配的"。

　　◀ match 的原义为"相配"。

❻ nervous：形容词，"紧张的"。

❼ doubt：动词，"怀疑"。

❽ pour cold water：动词词组，"泼冷水"。

What's next? 结果如何呢？

(They're in a famous jewelry store.)

Jessica: Look, sweetheart. These rings are gorgeous. It's not easy to pick one out.

Robert:　How about this one?

Jessica: It costs NT$32,000 dollars. Too expensive.

Robert:　Don't worry about the price. I can afford it.

Jessica: I don't want you to be in the hole before the wedding. Listen, now, we're in the same boat.

Robert:　You're really an angel.

（他们在一家知名的珠宝店。）

杰茜卡：看，甜心。这些戒指好漂亮，不知该选哪一个。

罗伯特：这个好不好？

杰茜卡：要新台币三万二。太贵了。

罗伯特：别担心价格。我可以负担得起。

杰茜卡：我可不想你在结婚前就负债。听着，我们现在可是在同一条船上，有难同当。

罗伯特：你跟天使一样善良。

Unit 14 如何开口套牢她
情境英语速成会话

必备活用单词

❶ pick out：动词词组，"挑选"。

❷ in the hole："负债"。

❸ in the same boat："同甘共苦"。

句型

What's on your mind?	你在想什么？

当我们看见别人有些心不在焉，或是有心事，便可拿出此句经典名言来套别人的话了。"on one's mind"有点类似放在心上；不过，有些人常把"What's on your mind?"和"in one's mind's eye"搞混了。"in one's mind's eye"是"脑海中、在想象中"的意思，是不是相差十万八千里呢？

这样说最地道！

婚姻（marriage）是人生的一大要事，从交往（date）、求婚（proposal）、订婚（engagement）、举行婚礼（wedding）、度蜜月（honeymoon），一路走来，可谓千辛万苦。不过，只要回想恋爱时的甜蜜，似乎一切辛苦都值得。可是，也有人说"匆忙结婚，悔恨终身"（marry in haste, and repent at leisure），搞到最后，竟以离婚（divorce）收场，真是浪费时间和精力。

这个单元的内容都记熟了吗？继续加油，准备前往下一个单元啰！

Unit 15
Let's go to a concert.
如何搭出租车&听音乐会

The wedding is approaching, and everyone is worried about them. However, Robert and Jessica will go to a concert to get rid of the pressure on them. Be quiet. The concert will start.

结婚迫在眉梢，别人都替他们两人简单的婚礼忧心不已，Robert 和 Jessica 却决定去听一场好听的音乐会，忘掉最近的忙碌。嘘，安静点！音乐会要开始了。

现在是什么情况?

(Robert and Jessica get into the cab, and he gives the taxi driver the address.)

Driver: To this address, sir?

Robert: Yes. How long does it take to get there?

Driver: It depends, but usually less than fifteen minutes.

Robert: We're in a hurry. Can you take the shortest way, please?

Driver: No problem. (Ten minutes later) Here we are!

Robert: Here is one hundred dollars and keep the change.

（罗伯特和杰茜卡进入出租车，他把地址交给司机。）

司　机：先生，到这个地址吗？

罗伯特：是。到那里需要多少时间？

司　机：看情况，不过通常不超过十五分钟。

罗伯特：我们赶时间。可以抄近路吗？

司　机：没问题。（十分钟后）我们到了。

罗伯特：这是一百元，不用找零。

(Robert and Jessica are at a concert. It's now the intermission.)

Jessica: Robert, wake up, wake up.

Robert: Is the concert over? Are we leaving?

Jessica: NO! It's intermission. You fell asleep 5 minutes after the concert started.

Robert: I'm sorry. I couldn't help it. When I listen to classical music, I always fall asleep.

Jessica: I'll bet if you were watching a hockey game, you'd behave very differently.

Robert: Well, we're just interested in different things.

（罗伯特和杰茜卡在音乐会上，现在是中场休息时间。）

杰茜卡：醒醒，快醒醒。

罗伯特：音乐会结束了吗？我们是不是要走了？

杰茜卡：不是！现在是中场休息。音乐会开始后五分钟你就呼呼大睡了。

罗伯特：对不起，我忍不住。当我听到古典音乐，我总是睡着。

杰茜卡：我打赌你要是看曲棍球比赛，情况一定会不一样。

罗伯特：哎，我们喜欢的东西不一样嘛！

必备活用单词

❶ cab：名词，"出租车"。

　　◀ 出租车的另一说法是 taxi；出租车司机称为 taxi driver。

❷ depend：动词，"看情形"。

　　◀ depend 原本是"依赖、依靠、信赖"之意；it depends 则有
　　　"看情形而定"的味道。

❸ change：名词，"零钱"。

　　◀ 此为不可数名词，所以不能用复数形式。

❹ intermission：名词，"中场休息"。

❺ hockey：名词，"曲棍球"。

　　◀ hockey game 为"曲棍球比赛"。

❻ behave：动词，"表现"。

What's next? 结果如何呢?

Robert:　Do you go in for classical music?

Jessica:　Sure. Classical music has so much more depth and
　　　　　meaning. I like the way it sounds.

Robert:　Then, what's your favorite piece?

Jessica:　Schubert's "Serenade", Tchaikovsky's "Sleeping Beauty", and Beethoven's 6th symphony.

Robert: You have a delicate ear for music.

Jessica: The performers seem at their best tonight. I hope you'll enjoy their performance.

罗伯特：你喜欢古典音乐吗？

杰茜卡：当然了。古典音乐既深奥又有深度。我喜欢它演奏的方式。

罗伯特：那，你最喜欢哪个曲目？

杰茜卡：舒伯特的《小夜曲》和柴可夫斯基的《睡美人》，还有贝多芬的第六号交响曲。

罗伯特：你很会欣赏音乐。

杰茜卡：今晚的演奏者演奏得淋漓尽致。我希望你能好好欣赏他们的演出。

 必备活用单词

❶ go in for：动词词组，"喜欢、参加"。

❷ classical music：名词，"古典音乐"。

❸ depth：名词，"深度"。

❹ piece：名词，"曲目"。

❺ serenade：名词，"小夜曲"。

❻ delicate：形容词，"精致的"。

❼ at one's best："最佳状况"。

 句型

| 1. How long does it take to ... | 需要多少时间…… |

询问到达某地需要多少时间，可以用"how long does it take from here to + 地点"。若要问某人做某事，需要费时多久，也可用此句型，只不过主语和宾语的地方得改变，例如："How long do you take to fix the bike?"（修好这辆自行车需要多少时间？）

| 2. at one's best | 最佳状态、全盛状态 |

此词组最容易和"do one's best"（尽全力）搞错。"at one's best"表示的是某人的最佳状态、全盛状态，例如我们常说某人的黄金时期，也可用此词组。现在，来比较一下这两个词组有什么不一样：我会尽力而为，英文是"I'll do my best."；"I'm at my best."（我处于最佳状态。）

这样说最地道！

对喜欢音乐（music）的人而言，听音乐是一大享受。音乐的种类繁多，比如说广受年轻人喜爱的瑞格（reggae）、大家耳熟能详的爵士乐（Jazz）、灵魂乐（soul music）、摇滚乐（Rock & Roll）、迪斯科（Disco）等等。可是并非所有的音乐都是美妙的音符，例如: face the music（面对现实、批评）、music to a person's ears（常指别人讨厌的声音，某人却觉得悦耳）。

 这个单元的内容都记熟了吗？继续加油，准备前往下一个单元啰！

Unit 16
The plots are all similar.
讨论电视节目

Robert and Luke don't go out on Friday night, so they invite some friends to come and drink some beer. There's only one TV in the living room. Men want to watch some programs and women others. What should they do?

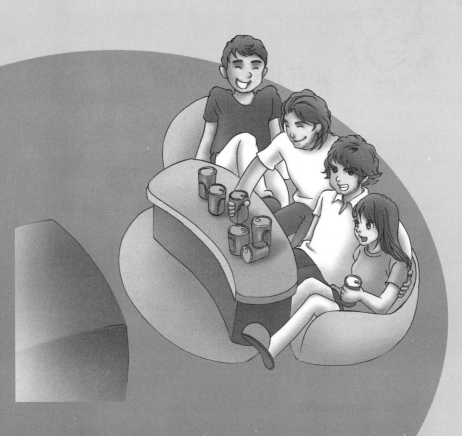

星期五晚上，Robert 和 Luke 没出去，便把几个朋友找来聚在一块喝啤酒。客厅只有一台电视，男人有男人喜欢的节目，女人有女人的。他们该如何是好？

 现在是什么情况?

Robert: What's showing on HBO now?

Linda: Let me see the TV guide. Oh, it's "Sex and the City", stories about the life of four girls living in New York.

Robert: I don't like the show. Can we find something else?

Linda: Why don't you like it?

Robert: The disgusting stories in "Sex and the City" are enough to turn my stomach. Besides, from a man's point of view, it isn't suitable for young girls like you.

Linda: Hey, come on. That's not fair.

 中文翻译

罗伯特：HBO现在在演什么?

琳　达：我来看看电视节目表。喔,是《欲望城市》,四个住在纽约女子的故事。

罗伯特：我不喜欢这部戏。可以看别的吗?

琳　达：为什么不喜欢呢?

罗伯特：《欲望城市》里讨人厌的故事令我倒尽胃口。还有,以男人的观点,那不适合像你们这样的女孩观赏。

琳　达：喂,别这样。真是不公平。

Jessica: What's your favorite TV program?

Luke: I like to watch the Japanese eating competition programs. They're very interesting and educational. How about you, Jessica?

Jessica: Recently, I've been watching a Korean TV series. They're so touching that I get tears in my eyes.

Luke: Girls always like to watch soap operas. I find the plots are all similar and boring.

Jessica: Watch your language. Girls here are staring at you.

杰茜卡：你喜欢什么样的电视节目？

卢　克：我喜欢看日本美食比赛的节目。它们非常有趣，又具有教育意义。你呢，杰茜卡？

杰茜卡：最近，我一直在看韩国电视剧。好感人喔！我都忍不住掉下眼泪。

卢　克：女孩就是喜欢看连续剧。我觉得情节都一样，也很无聊。

杰茜卡：注意你自己说的话。这里的女孩都在瞪你了。

必备活用单词

❶ TV guide: 名词，"电视节目表"。

◀ 一般的"时刻表、功课表"是 timetable；在美国 schedule 也有"时刻表、功课表"之意。

❷ disgusting: 形容词，"令人讨厌的"。

◀ 动词 disgust 有"令人讨厌"之意。

❸ turn one's stomach: 动词词组，"倒胃口"。

❹ point of view: 名词，"观点"。

◀ 等同于 viewpoint。

❺ suitable: 形容词，"合适的"。

❻ fair: 形容词，"公平的"。

◀ It's not fair. 是大家常挂在嘴上，用来抗议不公平的事件。

❼ competition: 名词，"竞赛"。

◀ 另一个表示"竞赛"的常用单词是 contest。

❽ educational: 形容词，"具有教育意义的"。

❾ series: 名词，"系列"。

⑩ soap opera：名词，"肥皂剧"。

◀ soap 原意是"香皂"；opera 是"歌剧"。

⑪ plot：名词，"情节"。

 ## What's next? 结果如何呢？

Rose: Can we change the channel?

Peter: Why? It's a funny movie, and he is an excellent actor.

Rose: You're telling me, but commercials on TV are really a nuisance.

Peter: I guess you're right. I don't like so much advertising, either.

Rose: There's too much violence on TV nowadays, too.

Peter: We should turn off the TV and go out to see a real movie.

罗　丝：我们可以转台吗？

彼　得：为什么？这部电影好好笑，他是不错的演员。

罗　丝：我知道，可是电视上的广告真令人讨厌。

彼　得：你说得没错。我也不喜欢这么多广告。

罗　丝：现在的电视充满了暴力。

彼　得：我们应该关掉电视，到外头看电影才对。

句型

I've been watching Korean TV series.	我最近一直在看韩剧。

现在完成时(have + p.p.)在语法中表示：

1) 从过去到现在为止已经做过、完成的动作。

2) 过去到现在有过或未曾有过的经验。

3) 从过去到现在一直持续的动作或状态。

例句中的语法称为现在完成进行时(have + been + V-ing)，多表示过去到最近的一段时间内，经常发生的动作、状态，或习惯性的动作。不难发现，现在完成进行时的语法结构，结合现在进行时和现在完成时，因此构成"have + been + V-ing"。例如："He's been telling me."（他一直跟我讲这件事情。）

这样说最地道！

看电视是许多人共有的经验，可是参观电视台（TV station）或电视摄影棚（TV studio）却不是，演艺圈（show business）因此便显得异常神秘。一般来说，演艺圈有些基本要素：导演（director）、摄影师（cameraman）、制作人（producer）、导播助理（assistant floor director）、剧本（script）、演员（actor / actress）、化妆师（make-up man）和观众（audience）等。

Unit 17
That was a close game.
谈论篮球

Women are so crazy about "Sex and the City" that men have to give up watching the other programs. They move to Robert's bedroom to watch TV. Basketball games are on the TV now. Without women bothering them, they can cheer for the team they like.

男人敌不过女人对《欲望城市》的喜爱，只好从客厅搬移到 Robert 的卧室。电视上正在上演美国NBA篮球赛，没有女人们打扰他们，他们可以替自己喜欢的队伍好好欢呼加油了。

现在是什么情况?

Robert: How is the game?

Luke: Both teams are tied at ten-all now. Last time the Lakers won the game by fifty to forty-nine.

Peter: Do you think San Antonio Spurs can win the championship back?

Robert: Perhaps the chances are against it.

Peter: If San Antonio Spurs want to win it back, they must work harder to win back.

Luke: Look, they gain the upper hand.

罗伯特：比赛进行得如何？

卢 克：两队以十分平手。上次湖人队以五十比四十九击败对手。

彼 得：你们认为马刺队可以把冠军宝座夺回来吗？

罗伯特：机会渺茫。

彼 得：要是马刺队想赢球，他们得更加卖力。

卢 克：看，他们占上风了。

(David Robison shot hoops on the TV. Five minutes later he wins.)

Robert: Go, David. Wow, what a dunk.

Luke: That was a close game. At the first, I didn't even dream of their winning this game.

Peter: David Robison's dunks and blocked shots have made him win.

Robert: I heard he is one of the best-paid and most popular basketball stars of the NBA.

Luke: It isn't money and fame that make him special. He donates money to help schools, needy children and the homeless.

· ·

（大卫·罗宾斯出现在电视上投篮。五分钟后他便赢了。）

罗伯特：大卫，快。哇，灌篮灌得太好了。

卢　　克：这场比赛真是有惊无险。起先，我还不敢想他们会赢得比赛。

彼　　得：大卫·罗宾斯的灌篮和盖帽让他赢得比赛。

罗伯特：听说他是NBA球员中薪资最高和最受欢迎的篮球明星之一。

卢　　克：不是钱和名声让他跟别人不一样。他捐钱帮助学校、有困难的孩子和无家可归的人。

Unit 17 谈论篮球
情境英语速成会话

必备活用单词

❶ tie：动词，"与……打成平手"。

◀ tie ten-all 为"全部都是十分打成平手"。

❷ ten-all："全部都是十分"。

❸ beat：动词，"打败"。

❹ champion：名词，"冠军"。

❺ against：介词，"不利于"。

❻ gain the upper hand："占上风"。

❼ shot hoops：动词，"投篮"。

◀ shoot 为 shot 的动词原形，有"投射"之意；hoop 是篮框。

❽ dunk："灌篮"。

◀ 有没有看过漫画 Slam Dunk（灌篮高手）呢？

❾ close game：名词，"势均力敌的比赛"。

◀ close 本身有"接近的、势均力敌的"之意。

❿ blocked shot：名词，"盖帽"。

◀ blocked 是"封锁的"之意。盖帽就是阻止别人投篮得分之意。

⑪ best-paid：形容词，"薪水很高的"。

　　◀ 其他相似的词还有 highly-paid。

⑫ fame：名词，"名声、名誉"。

　　◀ "有名的"就是 famous。

⑬ donate：动词，"捐款"。

⑭ needy：形容词，"贫穷的"。

　　◀ 表示贫穷的还有 poor, depressed。

⑮ homeless：形容词，"无家可归的"。

　　◀ 这类的形容词很多，大多是名词之后加上-less，如 careless(粗心大意的)、helpless(无助的)、harmless(无害的)。

What's next? 结果如何呢?

Peter:　Tomorrow is Saturday, and why don't we find some friends to play basketball?

Robert:　Good idea. I've watched everyone among us very closely, and I think Louis Yang is the best out there.

Luke:　I agree with you. Do you remember he was the one that scored the last 2 shots last time?

Robert:　And he knows how to take the initiative.

Unit 17 谈论篮球
情境英语速成会话

Peter: We should invite him to come with us.

Luke: But he's a family man now. Do you think he will waste
         his weekends with us?

彼　得：明天是星期六，我们何不找些朋友去打篮球呢？

罗伯特：好主意。我最近仔细观察我们这些人，我想路易斯·杨的
　　　　球技是我们当中最棒的。

卢　克：我同意你的看法。你还记得上次比赛中，他就是那个最后
　　　　投入两分反败为胜的人。

罗伯特：还有，他也知道如何先发制人。

彼　得：我们应该邀他跟我们一块去打球。

卢　克：但他现在是有家室的男人。你想，他会把周末的时间耗在
　　　　我们身上吗？

 句型

1. the best out there 　其中最棒的

我们常说某某东西是最棒的，通常只单纯使用best即可，如："He's
the best player."（他是最棒的球员。）；"The food here is best."
（这里的食物最棒了。）可是，当我们想表达某事物是其中最棒
的，就得用"S + V + the best out there."；或"S + V + the best

among + O" 了。如："Her singing is the best out there. = Her singing is the best among us." (她的歌声是我们当中最棒的。)

2. to take the initiative　先发制人

想要让某事出奇制胜，就得来个先发制人。例如:He took the initiative in making friends.（他主动跟别人交朋友。）

这样说最地道!

说到男人，不把他们和球类扯在一起真的很难，尤其是中国人对美国NBA篮球的疯狂。说到篮球，就让我们到篮球场（court）上看一场篮球赛（basketball game）吧！首先上场的是裁判（referee），然后是两队球员（basketball players）。突然，甲方一个攻击，来个空中接力灌篮（alley-oop）——得分（get points）。乙方不甘示弱，也投篮（shoot），可惜是篮外空心（air ball），连框（rim）都没碰到。

 这个单元的内容都记熟了吗？继续加油，准备前往下一个单元啰！

Unit 18
Hold your hands up.
抢劫怎么说&如何报案

Robert and some International classmates meet at the bar on Sunday night. After three o'clock they decide to go home. On his way to the MRT station, Robert is robbed. Fortunately, the police come as soon as possible.

星期天晚上，Robert 和几个外国同学相约在酒吧碰面。三点过后，大家各自回家了。当 Robert 准备搭捷运回家，却在路上遇到歹徒。幸好，警察很快就来了。

What's up? 现在是什么情况?

(One his way to the MRT station, a man is approaching to Robert.)

Stranger: Excuse me. Do you know where the address is?

Robert: Wait a minute. Let me see my map.

Stranger: Hold your hands up, and give me your wallet slowly.

Robert: Please don't take my wallet. My girlfriend's picture, credit cards, and friends' phone numbers are inside. I'll give you all the cash, OK?

Stranger: Shut up. Throw your wallet to me or I will kill you.

Robert: Whatever you say.

（去捷运站途中，有个人逐渐靠近罗伯特。）

陌生人：请问，你知道这个住址往哪儿走吗？

罗伯特：等一下。我查查我的地图。

陌生人：把手举起来，然后慢慢把你的皮夹交给我。

罗伯特：别把我的皮夹拿走。那里有我女朋友的照片、信用卡和朋友的电话号码。我会把所有现金给你，好吗？

陌生人：闭嘴。把你的皮夹扔给我，要不然，我就把你杀了。

罗伯特：一切都听你的。

(Robert calls and reports to the police officer.)

Police: Police station, may I help you?

Robert: I was robbed. How should I report it?

Police: Can you give me your name, where you were robbed, and how it happened, and how much you lost?

Robert: Sure. One thousand and my driver's license, student ID, and credit cards were all inside. Ma'am, do I need to go to the police station?

Police: Of course. There are some forms you need to fill out. Can you find the nearest police station and report it?

Robert: I don't think so.

（罗伯特跟警察报案。）

警　察：警察局，有什么我帮得上忙的吗?

罗伯特：我被抢了。我该怎么报案?

警　察：可以告诉我你的姓名、遇抢的地点、发生经过和你所损失的金额?

罗伯特：可以。一千块和我的驾驶执照、学生证和信用卡都在里头。警官，我得到警局一趟吗?

警　察：当然了。有些表格需要你来填写。你可以找到最近的警察局去报案吗?

罗伯特：好像没办法。

Unit 18 抢劫怎么说 & 如何报案
情境英语速成会话

必备活用单词

❶ approach：动词，"接近"。

❷ stranger：名词，"陌生人"。

❸ map：名词，"地图"。

❹ hold your hand up："把手举起来"。

❺ wallet：名词，"皮夹"。

　◀ 女用皮包称为 purse；一般的包包称为 bag。

❻ credit card：名词，"信用卡"。

❼ cash：名词，"现金"。

❽ incident：名词，"意外事件"。

❾ report：动词，"报告"。

❿ rob：动词，"抢劫"。

⓫ driver's license：名词，"驾照"。

⓬ student ID：名词，"学生证"。

What's next? 结果如何呢?

(Robert is in the police station, filling out a form.)

Police: When did it happen?

Robert: About half an hour ago. I was on my way to the MRT station, and a young man jumped out to ask me questions.

Police: Can you describe his appearance in simple Chinese?

Robert: Sorry, I'm afraid I can't make myself understood.

Police: It's all right. I'll find someone who can speak English and talk with you. Before my colleague comes, I think you'd better call your credit card company to cancel your credit cards.

Robert: That's true. The sooner, the better.

（罗伯特正在警察局填写表格。）

警　察：案件什么时候发生的?

罗伯特：半小时前。我正往捷运站途中，某个年轻人突然跳出来问路。

警　察：你可以用简单的中文描述歹徒的特征吗?

罗伯特：没办法，我怕我不能把我的意思明白传达出来。

警　察：没关系。我们会找个会说英文的人跟你谈谈。我的同事来之前，我想你最好打电话给你的信用卡公司，取消信用卡使用。

罗伯特：那倒是真的。而且是越快越好。

句型

I'm afraid that ... 　　　　　　恐怕……

英文中有许多委婉词，是怕直接的说话语气，可能会伤了对方脆弱的感情。这类的客气话，有时候会挑选一些 nice 的单词；有一些则是利用语法的特性来表示。听到"恐怕"，大家的印象好像是不好的事情即将发生，其实也不尽然，"I'm afraid (that) + 从句"就是一种婉转的拒绝、否定之意。若你的好朋友邀请你去看电影，你没空，可以说"I'm afraid I'm not free tonight"。这样，是不是清楚了些呢？

这样说最地道！

在美国，有许多称呼警察的名称：policeman, policewoman, police officer, the police, cop, law enforcement officer等等。中文的"警方"就是the police，此名词是集合名词，也就是明明是复数，却不用在名词后多加上s来表示复数。而影片中大家常见"条子"一词，就跟cop有点类似。说到警察的工作，好像全世界都大同小异，不是巡逻（patrol operations）、指挥交通（traffic control operations）、调查犯罪（investigations of crimes），就是处理爆炸物（bomb squad）。

Unit 19

Do you know how to inline skate?

如何描述运动 &
如何替别人加油

Robert, Jessica, Luke, and Rose have an important job to do tonight. They will attend an inline-skating contest held in an elementary school. Take a seat quickly, and cheer them on.

今晚 Robert、Jessica、Luke 和 Rose 四人可有个
重要的任务，他们要去参加一场在小学运动场举办
的直排轮比赛。快快快，坐下来。一起来替他们加
油吧！

现在是什么情况?

(Rose is a volunteer assistant working for Coach Tom.)

Rose: What should we do first, coach?

Coach: Come to check if the kids' pads are too tight or too loose.

Rose: OK. They need to wear pads properly to protect their elbows and knees.

Coach: Don't forget the helmets. You should help them adjust their buckles of the helmets.

Rose: No problem. I will do what you ask.

（罗丝是替汤姆教练工作的助理义工。）

罗　丝：我们首先得做什么，教练？

教　练：去检查孩子的护膝是否太紧或太松。

罗　丝：好的。他们需要把护膝穿戴正确以保护自己的手肘和膝盖。

教　练：别忘了那些安全帽。你得帮他们调整安全帽扣环。

罗　丝：没问题。你怎么说我就怎么做。

Jessica: Did you see that?

Robert: Yeah. I can't believe those kids pass through the bottles without difficulty.

Jessica: Oh, no. Jimmy had a tumble.

Robert: Not a big deal. He has been trained for some fundamentals so he can help himself up.

Jessica: You're right. Boys are boys. He did a good job.

杰茜卡：看见了吗？

罗伯特：看见了。真不敢相信那些孩子轻松地穿越那些瓶子。

杰茜卡：喔，不好了。吉米摔倒了。

罗伯特：没关系的。他已经受过一些基本动作训练，所以他可以自己站起来。

杰茜卡：你说得没错。男孩子就是男孩子。他表现得很好。

 ## 必备活用单词

❶ volunteer：形容词，"志愿的"。

◀ 名词型的 volunteer 表示"义工、自愿参加者、自愿军"的意思；表示自愿的动词也是同一个字，意思是"自愿做、自愿提供……"。

❷ coach：名词，"教练"。

◀ 教练顾名思义，就是提供指导和训练者，在运动场上，我们称"教练"为 coach 或 instructor；而其他的指导者可以称为：advisor、teacher、counselor、professor。

③ pad：名词，"护垫"。

◀ pad 除了当护垫外，还有"印泥、便笺簿"等意思。

④ properly：副词，"适当地"。

◀ 表示适当、合适的形容词有：proper、right、suitable、fitting。

⑤ helmet：名词，"安全帽"。

◀ 一般骑摩托车所用的安全帽，会用 motorcycle helmet；helmet 的本意是"头盔、钢盔"。

⑥ adjust：动词，"调整"。

◀ 表示"适应"的话，可用词组 adjust to...。

⑦ buckle：名词，"扣环"。

◀ 许多人会将 buckle 误认为衣服的扣子。衣服上的钮扣称作 button；而 buckle 是指扣环，如安全带、背包、安全帽上面的扣环。千万不要搞错了。

⑧ tumble：动词，"跌倒、栽跟斗"。

◀ 跌倒最常用词组 fall down；相关的词汇还有 trip（失足）、stumble（绊倒、踉跄）。

⑨ fundamental：名词，"基本动作"。

◀ 此外 fundamental 还有"基础的、重要的"之意。

What's next? 结果如何呢?

Robert: Do you know how to inline skate?

Jessica: No. Are there any basic techniques for inline-skating?

Robert: For the beginners, first, they have to know how to balance, control, and stop.

Jessica: It's not as complicated as skiing. And then?

Robert: After you learn how to stay in control, try to walk, slide, make a turn, or slow down.

Jessica: Oh, my. It's over my head. Why are these kids so good? Inline-skating is a piece of a cake to them.

罗伯特：你会溜直排轮吗？

杰茜卡：不会。溜直排轮需要什么基本技巧吗？

罗伯特：对于初学者，首先，他们得知道如何平衡、控制和停止。

杰茜卡：那不会比滑雪复杂。然后呢？

罗伯特：学会控制这些后，试着行走、滑行、转圈和减速。

杰茜卡：喔，老天爷。那已经超越我的能力所及。为什么那些小孩这么厉害？溜直排轮对他们是轻而易举。

必备活用单词

❶ inline skate：动词，"溜直排轮"。

❷ technique：名词，"技巧"。

❸ inline-skating：名词，"直排轮"。

❹ balance：动词，"平衡"。

❺ complicated：形容词，"复杂的"。

❻ slide：动词，"滑行"。

句型

| They need to wear pads properly to protect their elbows and knees. | 他们需要正确穿戴护具，以保护手肘和膝盖。 |

不定词的功用很多，它可以当名词、当宾语、当宾语补足语；这里，我们要介绍不定词当宾语补足语的用法。所谓宾语补足语，就是此补足语用来补充宾语的状态，使句子更加清楚。例如："they need to wear pads."只说明他们必须穿上护垫，并未说明护垫的

功用。可是，加上"to protect their elbows and knees"的时候，pads 的用处就十分明显了，喔，原来是为了(to)保护膝盖和手肘。所以，我们平常在句子看到不定词"to V"当宾语补足语(OC)，可以将它解释为"为了"，表示目的。

这样说最地道！

说到这 skating，许多人很容易搞混。还记得冬天穿着冰刀在湖上溜冰的景象吗？这种美妙的运动称为 ice skating；比赛用的花式溜冰则叫 figure skating；至于穿着笨重的四轮溜冰鞋的那种溜冰运动叫 roller skating；至于直排轮运动，有人称为 inline skating，那种鞋子称为 roller blades。

 这个单元的内容都记熟了吗？继续加油，准备前往下一个单元啰！

Unit 20
Give me a table in the non-smoking area.
如何订位&如何点菜

Robert wins a lottery, and the prize is five thousand dollars. He decides to treat his roommate and their girls. They go to a luxurious restaurant. They booked a table in the nonsmoking area, but the waitress takes them to a smoking area. What should they do now?

Robert 中了彩票五千美元。开心的他决定请他的室友和女孩们到餐厅大吃一顿。他们来到一家高级的餐厅，他们预约的位置明明是非吸烟区，带位的小姐却把他们带到吸烟区。这时，他们要怎么做呢？

现在是什么情况?

(Robert is making a dinner reservation by call.)

Robert: I'd like to make a reservation for dinner.

Staff: Yes, sir. What time will you be here?

Robert: This Friday night, around six.

Staff: How many people?

Robert: Six. Please give me a table in the non-smoking area.

Staff: No problem. May I have your name, please?

Robert: R-O-B-E-R-T.

（罗伯特正用电话预约晚餐位置。）

罗伯特：我想预约。

职　员：好的，先生。要预约几点？

罗伯特：这星期五晚上六点左右。

职　员：多少人？

罗伯特：六位。给我在非吸烟区的位置。

职　员：没问题。请问贵姓大名？

罗伯特：罗－伯－特。

(Robert and his friends are in the restaurant. The staff makes a mistake, so they are taken to the smoking area.)

Robert: Excuse me. We reserved a table in the non-smoking area.

Staff: Let me see the form. Sorry, sir. I'll change it for you immediately.

Robert: Do we have to wait for a long time?

Staff: It's hard to say, but I'll try my best.

Robert: We'll stay outside, and please tell us when the table is ready.

Staff: Sure. I'll find a seat with the best view for you.

（罗伯特和他的朋友在餐厅。餐厅员工搞错了，所以他们被带到吸烟区。）

罗伯特：不好意思，我们预订的位置在非吸烟区。

员　工：我来查看一下表格。对不起，先生。我会马上帮您换过来。

罗伯特：我们得等很久吗？

员　工：很难说，不过我会尽力而为。

罗伯特：我们会在外面等，位置弄好了请记得通知我们。

员　工：好的。我会替您找个景观最佳的位置。

Unit 20 如何订位 & 如何点菜
情境英语速成会话

必备活用单词

❶ reservation：名词，"订位"。

 ◀ make a reservation：适用于所有的订房、餐厅订位、电影票预约等。

❷ non-smoking area："非吸烟区"。

 ◀ non-是英文中常见的前缀，代表"非"之意。例如，文学中非小说类的书籍称为 non-fiction；不缩水的衣料称为 non-shrink。

❸ immediately：副词，"立刻"。

❹ try one's best：动词词组，"尽力而为"。

❺ view：名词，"景观"。

What's next? 结果如何呢？

Staff: Good evening, here is the menu. Would you like to have something to drink first?

Robert: Yes, Red wine, please. And two orange juices for the ladies.

Staff: Are you ready to order now, or should I come back later?

Robert: We want to order now. Four roast beef, one salmon, and one lamp chop.

Staff: Then, what kinds of salads and sauces?

Robert: Garlic pepper dressing and mushroom sauce. As for the salads, we all want asparagus. By the way, we'll order dessert after the meal.

员　工：晚安，这是您的菜单。想先喝点什么吗？

罗伯特：好，红酒。给两位女士橙汁。

员　工：准备好要点餐了吗？还是我等一会儿再过来？

罗伯特：我们现在可以点餐了，四份烤牛肉、一份三文鱼、一份羊排。

员　工：沙拉和酱料要哪一种？

罗伯特：蒜味胡椒和蘑菇口味。至于沙拉，我们想要芦笋。还有，用完餐后我们才要点甜点。

 句型

| 1. Are you ready to order now, or ... | 现在要点菜了，还是…… |

询问对方是否准备好进行某事，可以用 "Are you ready to + 动词原形"；或 "Are you ready for + 名词"。例如，问别人是否准备好要去游泳了，便可套用上面的用法 "Are you ready to swim?" 或 "Are you ready for swimming?"。

Unit 20 如何订位 & 如何点菜
情境英语速成会话

2. or 的用法

or 通常用在具有选择性的句子中，我们最常听见的例子就是"咖啡还是茶"(Coffee or tea?)。当别人提出选择性的问句时，我们不可用yes / no来回答，而是得直接提供答案。例如某人问："Do you like ice cream or pudding?"我们的答案就必须是两者都不要(I don't want any of them)、冰淇淋(ice cream)、布丁(pudding)、两者皆要（both）或任何一个都可以（either of them）。

这样说最地道！

除了豪华大饭店吃饭得预约外（make a reservation），上餐馆并不如想象中的难。由于太过便利了，我们对一些吃饭的过程却叫不出名字来。先是侍者（waiter/waitress）会来排好碗盘（set the table）、帮客人拉椅子（seat the customers）、倒水（pour the water）、客人开始点菜（order from the menu）、上菜（serve the meal）、清桌子（clear the table）、收走碗盘（carry the tray）、客人走向柜台付钱（pay the bill）、给小费（leave a tip）。

Unit 21
What qualifications have you got?
成功面试术

Robert will get married, so he has to find a part-time job to support their living expenses. He asks a lot of people about the techniques for interviews. Today a Miss Chen will interview him. Do you have any tips for successful interviews for him? Please tell him as soon as possible.

打算成家的 Robert，决定找份 Part-time 工作来支付日常生活开销。他问了许多人有关面试的技巧。今天他就要跟一位陈小姐面试了。你有什么面试必胜秘诀要送给他吗？现在赶紧跟他讲喔！

 现在是什么情况？

Chen: I've looked at your resume. Your background in furniture design is quite interesting. You say you want to apply for a part-time job as a furniture designer.

Robert: Yes. After I graduated from Chicago University, I was trained for that kind of job.

Chen: Have you ever thought about getting a full-time job?

Robert: Yes, but I'm a student now and taking a Chinese course in Taiwan University. I don't think I can manage school and a job well at the same time.

陈小姐：我看过你的履历。你在家具设计这方面的背景挺有趣的。你说你想要应征兼职家具设计师。

罗伯特：是的。从芝加哥大学毕业后，我便一直从事这类工作。

陈　姐：你不曾考虑做全职的工作吗？

罗伯特：想过了，可是我现在是学生，在台大修中文课。我想我无法同时把学业和工作处理好。

Chen: I'm sure you're qualified as a designer. But, as a part-time employee, the pay is not as high as you think.

Robert: I don't mind. Now I just need a chance.

Chen: Would you mind answering a few personal questions?

Robert: Definitely not.

Chen: According to your training and experience, you can find a high-paid job, but why do you give it up and study Chinese here?

Robert: I don't know. Maybe it's my destiny. You know, money is not everything. I have learned a lot and found my true love here.

陈小姐：你绝对符合设计师的工作。可是，作为兼职员工，薪水并不如你想象中的高。

罗伯特：我不介意。现在我要的只是机会。

陈小姐：你介意回答私人问题吗？

罗伯特：不介意。

陈小姐：根据你所受的训练和经验看来，你可以找一个高薪的工作，为什么要放弃，还来这里学中文？

罗伯特：我不知道。或许那就是我的命运。你知道的，金钱并不代表一切。我在这儿学到许多事情，也找到自己的真爱。

必备活用单词

❶ resume：名词，"履历表"。

❷ background：名词，"背景"。
　◀ background 除了是个人的身家背景之外，像是戏剧中的背景、照相时以花草为背景的背景，也是用这个单词。

❸ design：动词，"设计"。
　◀ designer 为设计师。

❹ apply for: 动词词组，"申请"。

❺ train: 动词，"训练"。

❻ manage: 动词，"处理"。
　◀ 看到这个字是不是觉得很眼熟呢？没错，英文的"经理"就是 manager，从manage 转变而来的。

❼ employee: 名词，"雇员"。

❽ give up: 动词词组，"放弃"。

❾ destiny: 名词，"命运"。

❿ for a living: 介词词组，"维生"。

⑪ article：名词，"文章"。

What's next? 结果如何呢？

Chen: What do you do for a living now?

Robert: I write some English articles for magazines.

Chen: I see. What company are you with now?

Robert: English Cool Kids, Joy Publishing Corporation, and so on.

Chen: Do you mind working overtime? Of course, we'll pay for it.

Robert: It sounds fine to me.

Chen: OK. I'll have to take you on a six month's probation first. I wonder if you'd mind starting next Monday?

Robert: No problem.

陈小姐：你现在做什么维生？

罗伯特：我替杂志写些英文文章。

陈小姐：我了解了。你现在替哪家公司工作？

罗伯特：诸如英语大王、如意文化等。

陈小姐：你介意加班吗？当然，我们会支付加班费。

罗伯特：听起来挺不错的。

陈小姐：好。我先给你六个月的试用期。你可以从下周一就来上班吗？

罗伯特：没问题。

必备活用单词

❶ and so on：副词词组，"等等"、"诸如此类"。

❷ work overtime：动词词组，"加班"。

❸ probation：名词，"试用期"。

句型

| What do you do for a living? | 你靠什么维生？ |

询问对方靠什么维生，转个脑筋想，就是询问对方目前的职业为何。What do you do for a living?也可解释为"你靠什么糊口？"或"你的工作为何？"不过，比较正式询问别人职业的问法是"What do you do?"、"What's your occupation?"等。

这样说最地道！

除了生老病死，许多人觉得找工作也算人生中的大事。工作能否录取，好像取决于履历表（resume）和面试（interview）时的表现。履历表除了记录个人资料（personal information）外，最重要的就是得把自己拿手的（professional）工作技能（job skill）好好展现出来，让雇主一看就动心，才能进阶到面试阶段。目前，最基本且必须具有的技能是英文能力（English ability）和电脑应用（operation of a computer）。至于面试，最重要的是必须穿着整洁（to wear neatly）、态度诚恳（honest and sincere），再来就是临场的机智反应（a quick mind）了。

这个单元的内容都记熟了吗？继续加油，准备前往下一个单元啰！

Unit 22
Shame on me!
如何表示责备

Finally, Robert finds a job. He works as an assistant designer for Miss Chen, a famous designer. On the first day, Robert is asked to look for information on the Internet by Miss Chen. Robert is not very good at computers. What should he do?

Robert 终于有工作了。他现在是一名台湾设计师的助理，她可是鼎鼎有名的设计师 Miss Chen。头一天上班，Miss Chen 就要 Robert 上网找资料，没想到他的电脑技能有点不太行。那该怎么办？

现在是什么情况?

(Robert is in Miss Chen's office. She needs Robert to do some work for her.)

Miss Chen: Please post these pictures on our website. Then, e-mail them to our clients.

Robert: Sorry, I don't know how to use the Internet.

Miss Chen: Unbelievable. In today's world, e-mail and the Internet are essential. I think you'd better learn it as soon as possible.

Robert: Yes. Anything else?

Miss Chen: (She makes a call) Wait! Tiffany will come here in a minute. She's our computer programmer, and she'd love to show you how to operate this machine.

Robert: Thanks, Miss Chen.

· ·

（罗伯特在陈小姐的办公室。她需要罗伯特帮她做点事。）

陈小姐：请把这些图片贴在我们的网站上。然后，将它们寄给客户。

罗伯特：抱歉，我不知道怎么使用网络。

陈小姐：太不可思议了。现今的工作，电子邮件和网络可是很重要的。我认为你最好赶紧学会。

罗伯特：好的。还有其他的事情吗？

陈小姐：（她打了通电话）等一下！蒂法妮等一下就来了。她是我们公司的电脑工程师，她会很乐意教你如何使用电脑。

罗伯特：谢谢，陈小姐。

Robert: Shame on me! I don't know how to use the Internet.

Tiffany: Don't blame yourself. Although we can't live without the Internet, it's never too late to learn.

Robert: Your words make me feel better. Where should we start?

Tiffany: I will give you some basic ideas about the computer: monitor, floppy disk drive, CD-ROM drive, keyboard, mouse, printer, modem, speaker.

Robert: I remember them all. What's next?

Tiffany: Turn on your computer first. See the sign? Click here twice. Welcome to the world of the Internet.

中文翻译

罗伯特：我实在太丢脸了！我竟不知道如何使用网络。

蒂法妮：别如此责备自己。虽然我们没有网络就无法存活，可是活到老学到老啊！

罗伯特：你的话让我好过些。我们从哪里开始？

蒂法妮：我会教你一些电脑的基本概念：显示器、磁盘驱动器、光

Unit 22 如何表示责备
情境英语速成会话

盘驱动器、键盘、鼠标、打印机、调制解调器、喇叭。

罗伯特：我全记住了。下一步？

蒂法妮：先开机。看见这符号了吗？点两下。欢迎来到网络世界。

 必备活用单词

❶ post：动词，"张贴"。

◀ 上网时常听见网友说 po 东西，这个 po 就是 post；而 poster
不是张贴者，是"海报"。

❷ website：名词，"网站"。

❸ client：名词，"客户"。

◀ 有关客户和客人，许多人会搞混。一般的顾客称为 customer；像
律师、大公司的客人，则称为 client。

❹ unbelievable：形容词，"太惊人的"。

◀ 说 unbelievable 多为因为对方做出的某事，太好或太糟糕的一
种感叹词。还有，也可用来表示某事不怎么符合逻辑的情绪用
词。

❺ essential：形容词，"基本的、重要的"。

❻ would better：动词词组，"最好"。

◀ 其缩写为 'd better，后接动词原形。

❼ programmer：名词，"程序设计师"。

❽ operate：动词，"操作"。

❾ blame：动词，"责备"。

❿ floppy：名词，口语的"磁盘"。

⓫ drive：名词，"机械的传动装置"。

⓬ click：动词，"点击"。

 What's next? 结果如何呢?

(After spending a whole week learning about the Internet, Robert is an expert now. He's discussing with Tiffany the role the Internet plays in everyone's life.)

Robert:　It can really be a lifesaver if it's used properly.

Tiffany:　You bet. Look at this article.

Robert:　"Using the Internet saves time and money because it cuts out a lot of unnecessary printing, posting, faxing, and phoning."

Tiffany:　What's more, when cruising the Web, you'll find everything you want, including a great vacation spot.

Robert:　Wow! When was your last vacation, Tiffany?

Tiffany:　Five years ago.

（花了整周时间来学网络，罗伯特现在可是专家了。他正在跟蒂法妮讨论网络在日常生活中所扮演的角色。）

罗伯特：若网络被适当使用，可说是救命的工具。

蒂法妮：当然了。看看这篇文章。

罗伯特："使用网络节省许多时间和金钱，因其省去了许多不必要的打印、邮寄、传真和打电话。"

蒂法妮：更重要的是，当浏览网站时，你会找到自己要找的任何东西，包括很棒的旅游景点。

罗伯特：哇！蒂法妮，你上一次度假是什么时候？

蒂法妮：五年前。

 ## 句型

Shame on me!	我实在太丢脸了！

表示自己做什么事情太过于丢脸，可用 "Shame on me!"。说别人做什么事情太过丢脸，则将 me 改成 you，如 "Shame on you!"。
"shame" 当名词使用时，表示 "羞耻、惭愧"，通常用来指责别人的错误，如："It's a shame for him to beat his wife."（他打老婆真是不要脸。）可是，"What a shame!" 不是指什么可耻的事，而是 "太可惜" 之意。

这样说最地道！

并非所有人都含着金汤匙出生，天生老板命，所以，想要飞黄腾达的人，还是从基层做起来得实在。说实话，给人打工也不简单，尤其是到那种只有两、三人的小公司上班，简直是要十八般武艺样样精通，举凡电话留言（to leave a message）、传真（to fax ）、打字（to type ）、复印文件（to make copies）、整理档案（to file papers）、推销（to sell），甚至营销（marketing）都得自己来。不过，苦归苦，那样反而比较容易学到东西喔！

 这个单元的内容都记熟了吗？继续加油，准备前往下一个单元啰！

Unit 22 如何表示责备
情境英语速成会话

Unit 23

It seems that the overhead projector is out of order.

东西坏了怎么办？

Miss Chen is going to give a presentation in front of her clients. She collects many slides and data for her clients. However, the overhead projector is out of order, so Robert finds someone to fix it. Hey, it's a good chance for Robert to be a hero.

今天Miss Chen 在客户面前做 presentation 时，她
准备了许多幻灯片和资料给客户。没想到投影机却
坏掉了，Robert 连忙找人来修理。这下子，Robert
成了个大英雄。

现在是什么情况?

(Chen's having trouble hooking the computer up to an overhead projector.)

Chen: Can you do me a favor?

Robert: Sure.

Chen: It seems that the overhead projector is out of order.

Robert: I'll take a look. I get it. You don't have the right adapter.

Chen: Thanks. Can you help me do this wiring?

Robert: When it comes to this stuff, you're asking the right person.

（陈小姐无法将电脑接上投影机。）

陈小姐：可以帮个忙吗?

罗伯特：当然。

陈小姐：投影机好像出故障了。

罗伯特：我来看看。找到了。你没有用对转接器。

陈小姐：谢了。可以帮我弄这些线路吗?

罗伯特：说到处理这些东西，你可是问对人了。

Chen: Then, how do I make it work?

Robert: Put the slides on the glass.

Chen: Robert, it's out of focus.

Robert: Don't worry. While I adjust it, you put the transparencies in order. Do you see the knob here?

Chen: Yes. What's it for?

Robert: It's the knob for adjusting. You just turn this knob right here where it says "focus."

· ·

陈小姐：接着，我该如何让它运作？

罗伯特：把幻灯片放在玻璃上。

陈小姐：罗伯特，没有聚焦。

罗伯特：别担心。当我调整焦距时，你把这些幻灯片依次序放好。看见按钮了吗？

陈小姐：看见了。那是做什么的？

罗伯特：那是用来调整的。你只要转动这个按钮到写着"焦点"的地方即可。

Unit 23 东西坏了怎么办？
情境英语速成会话

必备活用单词

❶ overhead projector：名词，"投影机"。

❷ out of order：副词词组，"失控、坏掉"。

❸ I get it："我找到了"。

❹ adaptor：名词，"转接器"。

❺ wiring：名词，"线路"。

❻ stuff：名词，"东西、物品"。

❼ slide：名词，"幻灯片"。

❽ glass：名词，"玻璃"。

❾ focus：动词，"聚焦"。

❿ adjust：动词，"调整"。

⓫ transparency：名词，"透明片、幻灯片"。

⓬ in order：副词词组，"按照次序地"。

⑬ knob：名词，"旋钮"。

What's next? 结果如何呢?

(The overhead projector in the office doesn't work again. Robert calls someone he knows in an appliance store to fix it.)

Robert:　Hi, Betty, it's me, Robert.

Betty:　Long time no see. Where have you been, Robert?

Robert:　Working. Listen, an overhead projector in my office is out of order. Can you find someone to fix it?

Betty:　What's the problem?

Robert:　Nothing happens when I press the "Play" button.

Betty:　O.K. I'll have one of our people go take a look at it.

（办公室里的投影机又出故障了。罗伯特打电话给电器店他认识的人来修理。）

罗伯特：嗨，贝蒂，是我，罗伯特。

贝　蒂：好久不见。你最近都跑哪去了，罗伯特？

罗伯特：工作。听着，我办公室的投影机坏了。可以找人来修吗？

贝　蒂：有什么问题？

罗伯特：我按"运行"钮，竟毫无动静。

贝　蒂：好。我会派我们的人去看看。

Unit 23 东西坏了怎么办?
情境英语速成会话

句型

Can you do me a favor? | 可以帮个忙吗？

出了问题，想请别人帮忙，可以用"Can you do me a favor?"；若想使语气更加婉转，就把Can改成Would，例如："Would you do me a favor?"就可以了。"Would you …"是所有"好口气"的万灵丹，只要加上它，没有礼貌的人也变得有礼貌了。请求帮忙，最近比较流行的有"Can you give me a hand?"。最普通的用法应该就是"Please help me."。

这样说最地道！

说起机器，真是让人头大。可是，不懂又不行，手指加上脚趾数数，办公室内的机器可不下十种。首先，每天都会碰上的打卡机（pinhole plotter），一进办公室门就会看见桌上琳琅满目的裁纸机（paper cutter）、旋转名片夹（rotary card file）、修正液（correction fluid）、大头针（pushpin）、回形针（paper clip）、钉书机（stapler），往脚底下一瞧，还有安全插头（surge protector）呢！

Unit 23 东西坏了怎么办?
情境英语速成会话

Unit 24
I'm calling in sick today.
如何跟公司请病假

Poor Robert. He has a high fever and a cough because of the flu. He is so weak that he almost can't get out of bed. He called in sick, and takes a good rest at home.

可怜的 Robert 得了流行性感冒，又是高烧又是咳嗽的。他虚弱得下不了床，他只好跟公司请假，待在家里好好休养一番。

 **现在是什么情况?**

Robert: This is Robert. May I speak to Miss Chen?

Tiffany: Sorry. Miss Chen isn't in yet. I'm Tiffany. Is there anything I can do for you?

Robert: Hi, Tiffany, I'm calling in sick today.

Tiffany: What's wrong? You looked fine yesterday.

Robert: I got the flu. I don't feel good.

Tiffany: But, you have a presentation this afternoon. It's very important to you and our company. Are you sure you want to miss it?

- -

罗伯特: 我是罗伯特。请问陈小姐在吗?

蒂法妮: 抱歉,陈小姐还没进办公室。我是蒂法妮。有什么需要帮忙的地方吗?

罗伯特: 嗨,蒂法妮,我今天打电话来请病假。

蒂法妮: 怎么了? 你昨天看起来好好的。

罗伯特: 我得了流行性感冒。我身体很不舒服。

蒂法妮: 可是,你今天下午有场说明会。那对你和公司都很重要。你确定要错过?

Robert: I'm so sorry, but I can't get out of the bed.

Tiffany: What bad luck. How are you planning and dealing with the presentation?

Robert: Mr. Wu will substitute for me.

Tiffany: Great. Do you want to leave a message for Miss Chen?

Robert: Sure. Tell her why I have to take the day off. Thanks.

Tiffany: Don't mention it.

罗伯特：我觉得很遗憾，可是，我无法下床。

蒂法妮：真倒霉。你要怎么处理说明会？

罗伯特：吴先生会代替我。

蒂法妮：太好了。你要留言给陈小姐吗？

罗伯特：好。告诉她我为什么非得请假不可。谢谢。

蒂法妮：小事一桩，别客气。

Unit 24 如何跟公司请病假

情境英语速成会话

必备活用单词

❶ call in sick：动词词组，"请病假"。

◀ 请假的用法很多，本例子即是其中之一。若是一般请假，而非病假，则可用"take the day off"。一般我们听见的"It's my day off."是指"今天我休假"，"day off"是休假的意思；而holiday中文翻译成"假期"，许多人以为请假可以用holiday来替代，那可跟请假相差十万八千里。

❷ flu：名词，"流行性感冒"。

◀ 表示生病可以用"get sick"；身体的病痛，在病痛前加上have即可，如"have a fever"（发烧）、"have a sore throat"（喉咙痛）、"have a headache"（头痛）、"have a stomachache"（胃痛）等。

❸ presentation：名词，"说明会"。

❹ get out of bed：动词词组，"下床"。

❺ substitute：动词，"取代"。

What's next? 结果如何呢?

(Chen is calling Robert with her cell phone, but the reception is really bad.)

Chen:　I got your message. Do you feel much better?

Robert:　Yes. Thanks for calling. How was the presentation?

Chen: Sorry, I can't hear you. Wait, I'll go somewhere else. Now I can hear you better. Yes, Mr. Wu did a good job.

Robert: Good for him. I'll be in as usual tomorrow.

Chen: Take it easy. See you tomorrow.

（陈小姐用手机打给罗伯特，可是信号非常差。）

陈小姐：我收到你的留言了。觉得好多了吗？

罗伯特：好多了。谢谢你打电话来。说明会进行得如何？

陈小姐：对不起，听不见。等一下，我到别的地方讲。现在听得比较清楚了。是，吴先生的表现很不错。

罗伯特：做得好。我明天会照常上班。

陈小姐：放轻松，好好休息。明天见了。

句型

Mr. Wu will substitute for me. 吴先生会代替我。

日常生活中我们常会用到"代替"这个词，却不知如何使用，最简单的便是"substitute for"，例如，"You can substitute margarine for butter."（你可以用人造奶油代替奶油），等同于被动的用法"Butter is substituted for margarine."。还有，也可以用"replace ... with"或词

组 "in place of" 来表示，其用法如下："You can replace butter with margarine."，其被动的表现手法为 "Butter is replaced by margarine."。而 "in place of" 是词组，不是动词，其用法通常在动词之后，如："You can use margarine in place of butter."。

 这样说最地道！

生病是很令人讨厌的。世界上，应该没有人喜欢生病吧！光想到那些瓶瓶罐罐和上医院的折磨，就会令人感到很痛苦。遇到小病，大抵上药房（pharmacy）拿些止痛药（pain killer）、感冒药（cold tablets）、咳嗽糖浆（cough syrup）、软膏（ointment）或眼药水（eyedrops）；大一点的病痛，就非得上医院打针（getting an injection）；严重的，可能还得卧病在床休息（get bed rest）。

Unit 24 如何跟公司请病假
情境英语速成会话

Unit 25
Do you know what the grand prize is?
如何描述尾牙&
如何描述抽奖

Wei-ya is coming, and the company is full of merriment. Tiffany has been telling Robert so much about drawings and annual bonus at the wei-ya. This is Robert's first time to go to a wei-ya, and he's looking forward to it.

尾牙快到了，公司笼罩在一片欢乐的气氛当中。听 Tiffany 讲得天花乱坠，Robert 第一次过尾牙，对于大家对尾牙抽奖和年终奖金的种种描述，充满了向往，希望尾牙赶快来。

现在是什么情况？

Tiffany: Our company's wei-ya is next Friday night. I'm so excited.

Robert: What for? It's just a common company dinner, isn't it?

Tiffany: Not exactly. What is a company dinner like in your country?

Robert: Like a company dinner. You know, nice food, good wine, ambitious business talk.

Tiffany: Wow! Sounds like the plots in a lousy movie. Don't you have drawings during the mealtime?

Robert: Never heard of it.

蒂法妮：下星期五晚上就是公司尾牙了。我好兴奋。

罗伯特：有什么好兴奋的？只不过是公司餐会而已，不是吗？

蒂法妮：才不是。在你的国家，公司餐会是什么样子？

罗伯特：就像公司餐会。你知道的，美酒佳肴、野心勃勃的商业对话。

蒂法妮：哇！听起来跟烂电影的情节没什么两样。你们用餐时间没有抽奖吗？

罗伯特：没听过。

Tiffany: It's your first Chinese New Year in Taiwan, so you
            don't have a clue. Wei-ya is a banquet with prizes,
            performances … you name it.

Robert: Amazing. Who can have those prizes?

Tiffany: Anyone who has good luck.

Robert: Do you know what the grand prize is this year?

Tiffany: A brand-new Toyota.

Robert: Toyota, I'm coming.

蒂法妮：这是你在台湾的第一个中国新年，所以你就不知道了。尾
        牙是有奖品、表演等等的餐宴。只要你说得出口，什么都
        有。

罗伯特：太神奇了。谁可以拿到奖品？

蒂法妮：好运的人。

罗伯特：你知道今年的头奖是什么吗？

蒂法妮：全新的 Toyota 汽车。

罗伯特：Toyota，我来啰！

必备活用单词

❶ company: 名词，"公司"。

❷ wine: 名词，"酒"。

◀ wine 大多指的是葡萄酒，一般我们会在 wine 之前加上颜色，如: white wine, red wine 来区分白酒和红酒。烈酒如威士忌、白兰地，我们称为 liquor；啤酒叫 beer。

❸ ambitious: 形容词，"野心勃勃的"。

❹ business talk: 名词，"生意经"。

◀ 生意经谈论的多是跟生意有关的对话。

❺ plot: 名词，"情节"。

❻ lousy: 形容词，"三流的、讨人厌的"。

◀ 说起 lousy 这个单词很有趣，它本身是"不洁的、满是虫子的"之意，可是我们也可用它来形容很俗的事物。例如某人穿了一件很俗的大花衬衫，我们就可以称那件衬衫为 lousy T-shirt。

❼ drawing: 名词，"抽奖"。

❽ mealtime: 名词，"用餐时间"。

⑨ prize：名词，"奖品"。

⑩ performance：名词，"表演"。

⑪ grand：形容词，"大的"。

⑫ brand-new：形容词，"崭新的"。

 What's next? 结果如何呢？

(After the dinner, they're going to do the first drawing.)

Tiffany:　It's for a microwave. Look, they're picking a name.

Robert:　Oh, no. It's Sue from accounting.

(Thirty minutes later.)

Tiffany:　Listen, here's the final drawing. The Toyota. Hold your breath.

Robert:　It's our last chance. Oh, no.

Tiffany:　I'm so miserable. The whole world is against me.

Robert:　Hey, cheer up. Every dog has its day.

（晚餐后，他们开始抽出第一个奖品。）

蒂法妮：奖品是微波炉。看，他们要抽出名字了。

罗伯特：喔，不会吧！得奖者是会计部的休。

（三十分钟后）

蒂法妮：听着，现在是最后的大奖了。Toyota，屏息以待吧！

罗伯特：这是我们的最后机会了。喔，不会吧！

蒂法妮：倒霉透了。整个世界都跟我作对。

罗伯特：嘿，开心点。风水轮流转，说不定下次轮到你。

 句型

You name it.	你尽管说、你说说看

name 本身有"提及、提出"之意，所以"You name it."就是你所提出的。当我们要举办 party，好朋友却突然问自己是否邀请了学校知名人物，这时，我们若说"You name it."（只要你说得出口），表示，只要你说得出口的大人物，我们都邀请了。这是"You name it."的第一种用法；另外，只要别人开口，我们都会办得到，也可用"You name it."这句子，如"If you need anything, anything at all, (you) just name it."（只要你需要帮忙，不管是什么，尽管提出来就是了。）

这样说最地道！

尾牙的乐趣，除了那天可以大吃大喝，看看餐桌转盘（lazy Susan）上的鸡头面向谁外，最重要的，就是抽奖（drawing）。特等奖谁都爱，可惜，幸运儿（a fortune's favorite）只有一个。到底是什么促成这些幸运儿鸿运当头（have all the breaks）呢？命运（fate）、时机（timing），还是运气（luck）？如果自己的八字（date of birth）不好，听说穿红色内衣裤（red underwear）可以加强好运。如果到头来还是没中奖的话，就把那套红色内衣当作安慰奖（consolation prize）吧！

这个单元的内容都记熟了吗？继续加油，准备前往下一个单元啰！

Unit 26
There are always ups and downs.
讨论职场沉浮

Luke works in an excellent computer company. Although the working hours are too long, the pay and the bonus is very high. Due to depression, the company is going to downsize. This streamlining has put a lot of people on edge. Luke is discussing it with his coworker.

Luke 在一家人人称羡的电脑公司上班，虽然工作时间有点过长，可是薪水、奖金非常高。由于经济不景气，最近公司准备缩编，整个办公室人心惶惶。Luke 和他的同事也在谈论这件事。

现在是什么情况?

Mina: Did you hear the rumor about downsizing?

Luke: Of course. This streamlining has put a lot of people on edge.

Mina: And morale seems to have hit rock bottom.

Luke: When'll our GM be back? She needs to give us an explanation.

Mina: She's returning tomorrow morning and there's been a meeting called for it.

Luke: I hope they won't pass the buck.

··

中文翻译

明　娜：你听说裁员的传闻了吗？

卢　克：听说了。这次缩编弄得人心惶惶。

明　娜：士气也降到谷底。

卢　克：总经理什么时候回来？她应该好好说明一下。

明　娜：她明天早上回来，还为此召开会议。

卢　克：希望他们不会推卸责任才好。

(The day after the meeting.)

Mina: I can't believe it. Management said we'd have to go through some difficult times for a deficit.

Luke: It has been called into question. I don't think we're really in the red.

Mina: What do you mean by that?

Luke: Have you ever seen the latest financial statement?

Mina: Yes. Oh, you've got the point. But why did they do this?

Luke: Maybe they don't want us to ask for a raise.

· ·

（开完会的第二天。）

明　娜：真不敢相信。主管说我们因赤字必须度过一段艰辛时期。

卢　克：挺令人质疑。我不相信我们亏损。

明　娜：你这么说是什么意思？

卢　克：你看过最新的财务报告了吗？

明　娜：看过了。喔，你说得有理。但他们为什么要这么做？

卢　克：或许他们不想我们提出加薪的要求。

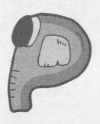

Unit 26 讨论职场沉浮
情境英语速成会话

必备活用单词

❶ the ups and downs："沉浮"。

❷ rumor：名词，"谣言"。

❸ downsize：动词，"裁员"。

❹ streamline：动词，"使有效率、现代化"。

　◀ streamlining 就是提高效率的动名词形态。

❺ put ... on edge：动词词组，"搞得人心惶惶"。

❻ morale：名词，"士气、品德"。

❼ hit rock bottom：动词词组，"降到最低点"。

❽ GM：名词，"总经理"。

　◀ GM 就是 general manager 总经理的缩写。

❾ explanation：名词，"解释"。

❿ call：动词，"召开"。

⓫ pass the buck：动词词组，"推卸责任"。

⑫ management：“上级，主管”。

⑬ go through：动词词组，“度过”。

⑭ deficit：名词，“赤字”。

⑮ in the red：“亏损”。

⑯ financial statement：名词，“财务报告”。

⑰ raise：名词，“加薪”。

 What's next? 结果如何呢?

Mina: I haven't seen Ken around lately. Has he left?

Luke: Yeah. He quit last week and found another job. He said he wasn't going to wait around worrying about whether or not the company was going to give him the boot.

Mina: Things haven't been the same around here since the last round of retrenchments. How is Ken doing?

Luke: Pretty good.

Mina: Everyone seems to be constantly run off their feet here.

Luke: Maybe we should map out the plan for our next jobs.

明　娜：我最近都没看见肯。他辞职了吗？

卢　克：是啊！他上周就辞职了，还找了别的工作。他说他才不要在这儿耗，担心公司是否要叫他走人。

明　娜：自从缩编后，这里就不太一样了。肯还好吧？

卢　克：非常好。

明　娜：大家最近都忙得不可开交了。

卢　克：或许我们该为下一个工作好好计划一下。

 必备活用单词

❶ quit：动词，"辞职"。

❷ boot：名词，"走路"。

❸ retrenchment：名词，"缩编"。

❹ constantly：副词，"不断地"。

❺ run of one's feet：动词词组，"忙得不可开交"。

❻ map out：动词词组，"为……详细拟订计划"。

句型

| Everyone seems to be constantly run off their feet here. | 大家最近都忙得不可开交。 |

想要表示"忙得不可开交"，可以用"run off one's feet"。例如本句，"Everyone seems to be constantly run off their feet here."，大家忙得停不下来，脚不沾地，是不是很生动呢？在本课之中，面临公司缩编的大环境，用这个词组可以达到"一石二鸟"的功效，一方面，说明公司裁员后员工减少，个人工作量相应增加，忙得不可开交。另一方面，也许很多人闻风而动，怕职位朝不保夕，忙着在外面找新工作。

这样说最地道！

景气不好（depression），失业率（unemployment rate）老居高不下。失业（unemployed）的朋友想要找工作，绝对要有永不放弃（never give up）的精神。首先，跟朋友谈谈（to talk to friends），或许他们能帮自己安插一个职务；或是到求职栏（to look at a job board）、报纸分类广告（to look in the classifieds）看看，说不定好运就向你报到。许多求职手册上教导求职新人，面试时一定要问清楚公司福利（to ask about benefits）、薪水高低（to inquire about the salary）等问题。其实，现在工作不好找，暂时骑驴找马，总有出头的一天（A dog has its day.）。

Unit 26 讨论职场沉浮
情境英语速成会话

Unit 27
I believe adaptability is a skill in itself.

如何要求加薪 &
打消下属加薪的念头

According to the company's announcement, those who aren't on the lists of the retrenchments must be curtailed of their salary. Luke can keep the job, but his salary will be cut down 20%. He thinks he works very hard, and shouldn't be treated like that. He tries to talk with his boss about a raise, but it isn't rosy.

根据公司正式宣布，不在缩编名单上的工作人员，必须依条件减薪。Luke 可以留在公司，不过薪水却减少百分之二十。他觉得自己工作非常努力，不应该获得如此对待。他找机会跟主管谈谈有关加薪的问题，结果并不理想。

现在是什么情况？

Luke: May I have a talk with you, Miss Yang?

GE: Go ahead.

Luke: I think everybody deserves a raise for all the extra work and hours we're putting in.

GE: You should have known that we have some financial difficulties because of depression.

Luke: I've heard of it.

GE: This is all part of going through the financial difficulties.

中文翻译

卢　克：杨小姐，可以跟你谈谈吗？

总经理：请说。

卢　克：因为我们额外的工作，还有我们投入的时间，我认为每个人应该加薪。

总经理：你应该知道，因为经济不景气，公司有些财务困难。

卢　克：我听说了。

总经理：这是渡过经济难关必经之路。

Luke: That theory doesn't hold water.

GE: Getting that pay raise helped lift spirits, didn't it?

Luke: Yes. Nobody likes having their wages reduced, and it keeps us on our toes.

GE: I believe adaptability is a skill in itself. It enhances your value to the company and gives you greater job security.

Luke: Sorry, I have to say I don't buy it.

....

卢　克：那理论行不通。

总经理：获得加薪真的有助于提升士气吗？

卢　克：是的。没人想要减薪，战战兢兢地工作。

总经理：我想适应本身是一项技能。它提升了你在公司的价值，因此也给予你更多工作保障。

卢　克：对不起，我无法接受。

必备活用单词

❶ deserve：动词，"应得"。

◀ 此单词用在坏的方面，最常出现在 "Someone deserves it." 这个句子里，表示"罪有应得、活该"，如某人考试作弊被开除了，可以说是 "He deserves it."；可是，"Someone deserves it." 也可用在好的方面，表示某人"应得此奖赏、功劳"等等。所以，要看情况使用。

❷ extra：形容词，"额外的"。

❸ put in：动词词组，"投入、提出"。

❹ because of：副词词组，"因为"。

◀ because of 和 because 不同的地方在于，of 是介词，所以不能接句子，只能接名词或动名词。

❺ depression：名词，"经济不景气"。

❻ theory：名词，"理论"。

❼ hold water：动词词组，"合情合理"。

❽ lift：动词，"提升"。

❾ spirit：名词，"精神、士气"。

❿ reduce：动词，"减少、降低"。

⓫ wage：名词，"薪水"。

⓬ put one on one's toes：动词词组，"胆战心惊"。

⓭ adaptability：名词，"适应能力"。

⓮ enhance：动词，"强化、加强"。

⓯ security：名词，"保障、安全感"。

What's next? 结果如何呢？

GE: Luke, don't you think you have some attitude problems.

Luke: I don't mean to offend or argue with you, Miss Yang, but I'm just striving for what we deserve.

GE: I hope you all can understand that profits are down, and retrenchments are to be expected.

Luke: So, we have nothing in common on this issue.

GE: I'm afraid not.

中文翻译

总经理：卢克，难道你不觉得自己的态度很不好吗？

卢　克：杨小姐，我无意冒犯或跟你争辩，我只是为自己争取应得的权利。

总经理：我希望你们可以理解，获利下降，缩减经费是可以预期的。

卢　克：那在这个议题上，我们没有共同点了。

总经理：恐怕的确是如此。

句型

Your theory doesn't hold water. 你的理论不合情理。

通常我们说"Your theory doesn't hold water.",大多表示不同意、反对对方的话。"hold water"有"合理"之意,所以表示某事不合情理,可以说"It doesn't hold water.";若是合乎情理,直接用肯定句"It holds water."即可。而"It doesn't make sense."跟本例句有异曲同工之妙,不同的是,"It doesn't make sense."大多用来表示超乎常理的事情。

这样说最地道!

明明自己替公司做牛做马(work like a slave),不像有人浑水摸鱼(slacking),只靠着拍马屁(kiss up to the boss)就官运亨通,那样的上司(supervisor)好像瞎了眼的昏君;想要忍下这口气,让身旁的小人得道,好像对自己有点残忍;可是,跑到上司面前摆明要晋升(promotion),又有点尴尬(embarrassing)。万一提议被打了回票,又丢了工作,不是赔了夫人又折兵吗?有一个船过水无痕的方法——暗示(to give him a hint)。有意无意地暗示,让老板明白自己劳苦功高,应该挺有效的。

Unit 27 如何要求加薪&
打消下属加薪的念头
情境英语速成会话

Unit 28
This is my resignation.
如何说明离职原因

After communicating with Miss Yang several times, Luke decides to quit, because the company won't change its policy. To buy a house and pay for the first down payment, Luke has to find a job with higher pay. He knocks at Miss Yang's door, and is going to give her his resignation.

和主管 Miss Yang 沟通了几次后，公司方面不会改变策略，于是 Luke 决定要辞职。他为了买房子和缴首付款，决定辞职找薪水高一点的工作。Luke 敲了 Miss Yang 的门，准备递交他的辞职信。

现在是什么情况?

Luke: Miss Yang, may I borrow a minute of your time and have a talk with you?

GM: Sure. Go ahead.

Luke: After a long consideration, I have decided to resign.

GM: Are you positive?

Luke: Yes. This is my resignation. Personally, I agree with the company's principle, but I might have some problems if I stay.

GM: Could you tell me what problems?

....

中文翻译

卢　克：杨小姐，可以借几分钟说话吗?

总经理：当然，请便。

卢　克：经过长时间的考虑后，我决定辞职。

总经理：当真?

卢　克：是的。这是我的辞呈。私底下，我是赞同公司的方针，可是我若继续留下，可能有些难题。

总经理：可以告诉我是哪些难题吗?

Luke:	I'm buying a three-bedroom apartment next year, so I've been saving money for the first down payment.
GM:	Congratulations.
Luke:	My salary, you know, it's not enough to cover the apartment's installment and my living expenses.
GM:	I see, but I really can't help.
Luke:	I understand your situation
GM:	Thanks.

中文翻译

卢　克：我明年要买三房的公寓，所以我一直存钱筹首付款。

总经理：恭喜。

卢　克：我的薪水，你知道，根本不够付公寓的分期付款和生活费。

总经理：我知道，可是我也无能为力。

卢　克：我理解你的处境。

总经理：谢谢。

必备活用单词

❶ consideration：名词，"考虑"。

◀ consideration 是由动词 consider 转变而来，表示经过深思的考虑。跟 consideration 有关的句子、词组还挺多的，例如："That's a consideration."（那是值得考虑的问题、事情。），此处的 consideration 有"因素、理由"之意；"I didn't tell her the truth out of the consideration for her feelings."（为了顾及她的情感，我没将实情告知。），此处的"out of the consideration for"是"顾念"之意。

❷ resign：动词，"辞职"。

❸ positive：形容词，"肯定的、积极的"。

❹ resignation：名词，"辞呈"。

❺ personally：副词，"私底下"。

❻ principle：名词，"方针"。

❼ save money for：动词词组，"为……而存钱"。

❽ down payment：名词，"首付款"。

❾ situation：名词，"情况"。

我们常说在某种情境下，我会怎样怎样，这个情境英文就是 situation。跟 situation 有关的词组比较少，常用的是 save the situation（拯救情势）。

What's next? 结果如何呢?

GM: So, when are you going to leave?

Luke: As soon as you find someone to replace my position.

GM: I see. It's being wonderful working with you.

Luke: You, too.

GM: After all of these, I hope we can still be friends.

Luke: You bet.

总经理：那你何时要离开呢？

卢　克：只要你一找到替代我的人。

总经理：我了解了。跟你共事很愉快。

卢　克：我也是。

总经理：经过这些事情，希望我们还能当朋友。

卢　克：当然可以。

句型

| As soon as you find someone to replace my position. | 一旦你找到替代我的人。 |

英文中有许多"一旦",如:"as soon as"和"once",两者都是连接词,可以用来连接两个句子。除了表示"一旦"外,本句中as soon as,也有别的解释,如"只要"。"I will get married as soon as I find someone I love."(只要我找到喜欢的人,我就会结婚)。此外,"as soon as"跟"possible"和"you can"搭配,就不再具有此意思,而是表示"尽快"之意,如:"I will go there as soon as possible. = I will go there as soon as I can."(我会尽快赶过去。)

这样说最地道!

职场(working field)上高超的EQ大王应该是Miss Yang这样的人物,也难怪她会年纪轻轻就当上总经理(general manager)的职务(position)。人家说职场如战场(battle),可是,也没有永远的敌人(enemy)和朋友;就跟小人(narrow-minded people)一样。许多算命老师告诫年轻人一句话,小人长在嘴巴上。意思就是,因为我们的快人快语(straight from the shoulder),往往不经意得罪(offend)别人而不自知,自然就产生了小人。因此,我们纵有天资英才,在行事风格上,如能尽量顾及他人、内敛一点,自能如道家所说"退一步海阔天空"了。

Unit 29
You are a natural born boss.
如何谈论事业

Lily is Luke's senior high school classmate. She was an engineer three years ago, but because of her new plan for life, Lily bought a franchise, running her own business. Her salary is higher than most white-collar workers. To see if he is right for being a boss, Luke contacts her and asks for information about franchising.

Lily 是 Luke 的高中同学。三年前，她也是一名工程师。由于新的人生计划，Lily 开始经营加盟店，当起老板来。她的薪水比一般白领阶层还要高。Luke 和她取得联系，希望对她的工作有更多了解，看看自己是否适合当老板。

 **现在是什么情况?**

(Luke comes to visit Lily.)

Luke: Hi, Lily. Long time no see. How are you doing?

Lily: Pretty good, thanks. What brings you here?

Luke: I quit my job a month ago. I'm considering purchasing a franchise, but I'm afraid of the hidden risks in them. So, I think I'd better pick your brains.

Lily: I'm flattered. Well, before you get your feet wet, have you ever asked yourself why you picked out the franchise, but nothing else?

(卢克前往拜访莉莉。)

卢克: 嗨, 莉莉。好久不见。近来好吗?

莉莉: 很不错, 谢谢。什么风把你吹来?

卢克: 一个月前我把工作辞了。我想经营加盟店, 可是我担心背后的风险。所以, 我想我最好听听你的意见。

莉莉: 我受宠若惊。好吧, 在你涉足之前, 你曾问过自己为何挑选加盟, 而非其他的事业吗?

Luke: You got me! All I want just is to earn some money from my apartment's down payment.

Lily: That's all? Running a business needs ambition and patience.

Luke: Good. Let me think. I want to have my own career.

Lily: That's better. Do you like to get along with people?

Luke: Does it have anything to do with running a franchise?

Lily: Definitely. Read the questionnaires on this magazine from the Chamber of Commerce.

Luke: (Five minutes after reading the magazine) I'm a type A person, so it means I have an easygoing personality. I don't understand, Lily, why does my personality have to be counted into it?

Lily: It's a long story, but let me cut it short. What kind of vendors do you prefer: an easygoing one or a dump one?

Luke: I see.

· ·

卢克：你可问倒我了。我想做的只是赚钱付公寓的首付款。

莉莉：就这样？经营事业需要野心和耐心。

卢克：好。让我想想。我想要拥有自己的事业。

莉莉：比刚才好多了。你喜欢跟人相处吗？

卢克：那跟经营加盟店有什么关系？

莉莉：绝对有。读读这份来自商业杂志的问卷调查。

Unit 29 如何谈论事业
情境英语速成会话

卢克：（读完杂志后的五分钟）我是A型，那表示我的个性很容易和人相处。我不懂，莉莉，为何我的个性也跟这有关？

莉莉：说来话长，我就长话短说啦！你比较喜欢哪种小贩：个性随和的，还是寡言木讷的？

卢克：我懂了。

 ## 必备活用单词

❶ purchase：动词，"购买"。

❷ franchise：名词，"加盟"。

❸ hidden：形容词，"隐藏的"。

❹ risk：名词，"危机"。

❺ pick one's brains：动词词组，"学习某人的聪明才智"。

❻ flatter：动词，"谄媚、奉承、使高兴"。

❼ get one's feet wet：动词词组，"涉足、涉入"。

❽ pick out：动词词组，"挑选出"。

⑨ earn：动词，"赚取"。

⑩ patient：名词，"耐心"。

⑪ career：名词，"事业、生涯"。

⑫ get along with：动词词组，"和人相处"。

⑬ questionnaire：名词，"问卷"。

⑭ chamber of commerce：名词，"商会"。

⑮ type A person：名词，"A型的人"。

⑯ easygoing：形容词，"个性随和的、易相处的"。

⑰ personality：名词，"个性"。

⑱ count into：动词词组，"把……计算在内"。

⑲ cut short：动词词组，"缩短"。
◀ cut it short 就是"长话短说"之意。

⑳ vendor：名词，"小贩"。

21 dump：形容词，"木讷的"。

What's next? 结果如何呢?

Luke: What gave you so much confidence to start the franchise?

Lily: Well, before I started in, I had investigated all franchises in Taiwan thoroughly.

Luke: Where did you get the information?

Lily: You can look for it in some financial magazines. Oh, don't skip some reliable rating guides to evaluate those owners' performance in the indexes.

Luke: OK, I'll remember that.

卢克：什么让你产生自信开始经营加盟店？

莉莉：事实上，在我开始之前，我已经把台湾所有加盟体系调查得一清二楚。

卢克：你从什么地方拿到这些资料？

莉莉：你可以在财经杂志拿到这些资讯。喔，别略过那些附于书后的指南，用来替经营者表现评分的可靠评比。

卢克：好的，我会记得。

句型

I'm considering purchasing a franchise | 我正考虑要做加盟生意

以前我们已经学过consider（考虑），而表示正考虑要做某件事，可以用固定句型"consider + V-ing"。例如："She considered writing a book about a blind woman, but she gave up."（她考虑写本跟盲女有关的书籍，可是放弃了。）许多人会将本例句中的considering和介词的considering搞混。介词的considering意思是"鉴于、就……而论"，如"She looks young considering her age."（就她的年纪而言，她看起来挺年轻的。）此处的considering跟consider成了现在分词considering不一样的用法。

这样说最地道！

以前常听老一辈的人（the elder）说：生意子（businessman）难生。意思是说天生拥有商人头脑（commercial spirit）的人很少。做过生意的人铁定很同意这句话。做生意确实不简单，对内，得学会采购（to purchase）、控制成本（to control prime cost）、定价格（to price）、行销技巧（salesmanship）；对外，随时和客户保持互动、聆听抱怨（to listen to compliant）、微笑（to smile）、真诚（to be sincere）、甜言蜜语（to be honey-mouthed）。即使对方是难缠的客人（bad customers），依旧不能动怒（to lose one's temper）。

Unit 30
I will win their hearts.
如何成功借钱

After long consideration, Luke decides to run a shop. He himself not only likes drinking coffee, but also has researched coffee thoroughly. Therefore, he wants to have his own coffee shop. He doesn't have enough money, so he'll have to get a loan from a bank. Today he walks into the bank with his business plan for the coffee shop as well as a smile. When he walked out of the bank, he knows he will find his way.

经过一番考虑后，Luke 也决定自己当老板。他喜欢喝咖啡，对咖啡又特别有研究，所以决定开一家咖啡厅。不过，他的资金不够，他得找家银行贷款。今天他带着自己的开店企划书和一脸的笑容，走进了银行。当他开心地走出银行大门时，他知道自己找到自己的路了。

现在是什么情况？

(Luke spends several hours writing his business plan. He is talking to Rose.)

Luke: Can you do me a favor, Rose? I need someone to give me some advice about my business plan.

Rose: It's my pleasure. There are two parts to your executive summary: general summary and financial projections.

Luke: In the first part, I introduce my company's goals, its products and services. To make it perfect, I list its target market.

（卢克花了好几小时写他的商业计划书。他现在正跟罗丝说话。）

卢克：罗丝，帮我个忙，好吗？我需要有人给我的商业计划书提点意见。

罗丝：那是我的荣幸。你的执行大纲有两部分：总论和财务评估。

卢克：第一部分，我介绍公司目标、产品和服务项目。为了使它更加完美，我列了其目标市场。

Rose:	In the second part, you have some realistic figures about the company's profit potential. Your management team is very professional and reliable.
Luke:	If you were a banker, could I have a loan?
Rose:	Um, your executive summary is excellent. I think it can grab the reader's attention and money.
Rose:	What will you wear to the loan interview?
Luke:	A T-shirt and jeans.
Rose:	Hey, you're going to see a banker, not go on a picnic.
Luke:	What should I do, then?
Rose:	A first impression is very crucial, so you should wear a formal dress. Keep it in mind: you never get a second chance to make another first impression.
Luke:	I get it. All right, I will wear my best tuxedo and a sincere smile.
Rose:	Trust me. You'll win their hearts.

中文翻译

罗丝：第二部分，你就公司的可能利润提出实际的数字。你的管理
团队非常专业和可靠。

卢克：你要是银行家，会贷款给我吗？

罗丝：嗯，你的执行大纲太棒了。我想那可获得阅读者的注意和金
钱。

罗丝：贷款面试那天，你要穿什么样的衣服？

卢克：衬衫和牛仔裤。

Unit 30 如何成功借钱
情境英语速成会话

罗丝：嘿，你是要去见银行家，不是要去野餐。

卢克：那我该怎么做？

罗丝：第一印象非常重要，所以你该穿正式一点的衣服。记得：你
没有第二个机会再来一个第一印象了。

卢克：我明白了。好吧！我会穿上最好的西装和带着诚恳的笑容。

罗丝：相信我，你会赢得他们的心。

 必备活用单词

❶ business plan：名词，"商业计划书"。

❷ it's my pleasure："那是我的荣幸"。

❸ executive：形容词，"执行的、行政的"。

❹ summary：名词，"简介、摘要"。

❺ general：形容词，"大体的、概要的"。

❻ projection：名词，"评估"。

❼ introduce：动词，"介绍"。

❽ goal：名词，"目标"。

❾ target：名词，"欲达到的目标"。

❿ realistic：形容词，"实际的、真实的"。

⓫ figure：名词，"数据"。

⓬ profit：名词，"利润"。

⓭ potential：形容词，"有潜力的"。

⓮ management：名词，"管理、经营"。

⓯ professional：形容词，"专业的"。

⓰ reliable：形容词，"可信赖的"。

⓱ grab：动词，"攫取"。

⓲ loan：名词，"贷款"。

⓳ jeans：名词，"牛仔裤"。

⓴ banker：名词，"银行家"。

㉑ impression：名词，"印象"。

Unit 30 如何成功借钱
情境英语速成会话

㉒ crucial：形容词，"关键的、重要的"。

㉓ formal：形容词，"正式的"。

 What's next? 结果如何呢?

(Mary Luo works in the loan apartment. She's going to see Luke.)

Mary: Nice personal touch. Mr. Chen, you have a wonderful business plan.

Luke: Thanks. I just tried my best. So, the loan…

Mary: Everything you represent qualifies the standards, and who can reject it?

Luke: What a relief!

Mary: Congratulations, Mr. Chen.

（罗玛丽在贷款部门工作。她将要接见卢克。）

玛丽：令人感动。陈先生，你的商业计划书写得太好了。

卢克：谢谢。我只是尽力而为。所以，贷款……

玛丽：你所提出的都符合我们的标准，谁可以拒绝你呢？

卢克：我可是松了一口气。

玛丽：恭喜，陈先生。

句型

What a relief!	真是松了一口气！

中文里头有许多词汇用来表示惊讶、感叹的情绪，英文中也有。不过，英文的表现手法是透过文法来呈现情绪的起伏。最常见的感叹句就是由 what 所引导的句子，其句型多为"What + a + 单数名词"，如："What a nice girl!"（真是个好女孩!）；通常由 what 所引导的句子也等同以how所引导的句子，不同的是，what 后面多跟着名词，how 则是强调形容词，如："How nice the girl is!" = "What a nice girl!"

这样说最地道！

故事中的 Mary 在贷款部门（loan department）工作，她的办公室位于银行的二楼。上了楼梯，一进门，柜台上清楚可见"贷款信用部"的蓝色牌子，这个位置，同时也是贷款付款窗口（loan payment window）。玛丽的职位是贷款授信人（loan record keeper），专门接见贷款者（loaner），审核（to verify）他们的资格（qualification）。还有，银行的经理（manager）和副理（administrator）也会审核贷款者的信用（credit）。至于放款，Luke就应该找贷款出纳员（loan teller）了。

Unit 30 如何成功借钱
情境英语速成会话

图书在版编目(CIP)数据

　　情境英语速成会话(含MP3光盘)/萧珮编著. —上海：华东理工大学出版社，
2010. 1

　　ISBN 978-7-5628-2637-8

　　Ⅰ.情… Ⅱ.萧… Ⅲ.英语—口语 Ⅳ. H319.9

　　中国版本图书馆CIP数据核字(2009)第175900号

本书由(台湾)三思堂文化事业股份有限公司授权华东
理工大学出版社在中国大陆地区以简体字出版发行

著作权合同登记号："图字: 09-2008-134号"

情境英语速成会话 (含MP3光盘)

编　　著 / 萧　珮
策划编辑 / 王耀峰
责任编辑 / 曹慧炜
责任校对 / 李　晔
封面设计 / 陆丽君
出版发行 / 华东理工大学出版社
　　　　　　地址: 上海市梅陇路130号，200237
　　　　　　电话: (021)64250303(营销部)
　　　　　　　　　 (021)64251904(编辑室)
　　　　　　传真: (021)64252707
　　　　　　网址: press.ecust.edu.cn
印　　刷 / 江苏句容市排印厂
开　　本 / 890mm×1240mm　1/32
印　　张 / 7.875
字　　数 / 225千字
版　　次 / 2010年1月第1版
印　　次 / 2010年1月第1次
印　　数 / 1-6000册
书　　号 / ISBN 978-7-5628-2637-8/H・869
定　　价 / 28.00元（含MP3光盘）

(本书如有印装质量问题，请到出版社营销部调换。)